"It would seem that we're stuck with each other."

Fergus's choice of words annoyed Noelle. "We most certainly are not!" she retorted. "There's no way I'll agree to share a home with you."

"How can you avoid it? You heard the terms of the will." Fergus seemed to taunt her.

"You could buy me out," Noelle suggested coolly.

"Impossible! We'll just have to put up with each other." Fergus met her gaze. "Of course," he added slowly, "the most obvious solution is for us to get married. Then our interests would be mutual."

Noelle could barely conceal the panic she felt at Fergus's words . . . or understand the excitement.

ANNABEL MURRAY has pursued many hobbies. She helped found an arts group in Liverpool, England, where she lives with her husband and two daughters. She loves drama: she appeared in many stage productions and went on to write an award-winning historical play. She uses all her experiences—holidays being no exception—to flesh out her character's backgrounds and create believable settings for her romance novels.

Books by Annabel Murray

HARLEQUIN ROMANCE
2549—ROOTS OF HEAVEN
2558—KEEGAN'S KINGDOM
2596—THE CHRYSANTHEMUM AND THE SWORD
2612—VILLA OF VENGEANCE
2625—DEAR GREEN ISLE
2717—THE COTSWOLD LION
2782—THE PLUMED SERPENT
2819—WILD FOR TO HOLD

HARLEQUIN PRESENTS
933—LAND OF THUNDER
972—FANTASY WOMAN

Ring
of Claddagh
Annabel Murray

Harlequin Books

TORONTO • NEW YORK • LONDON
AMSTERDAM • PARIS • SYDNEY • HAMBURG
STOCKHOLM • ATHENS • TOKYO • MILAN

Original hardcover edition published in 1986
by Mills & Boon Limited

ISBN 0-373-02843-1

Harlequin Romance first edition June 1987

CHAPTER ONE

'I STILL can't believe it.' Somehow Noelle felt impelled to break the silence, as she and her uncle lingered, unwilling to leave the quiet Suffolk graveyard and the woman, beloved of them both, who had just been laid to rest. 'It all seemed to happen so suddenly,' she went on, 'one day Liz seemed her usual self, the next day she was ill, a week later . . . dead.'

John Madox-Browne swallowed painfully before he was able to answer her.

'That was the way your aunt wanted it. She'd known, we'd both known for some time, that her heart wasn't too good. She didn't want you worrying, especially as you were so busy and happy.'

'Don't!' Noelle winced, her blue eyes filling with tears. 'It makes me feel unutterably selfish. I should have known, should have noticed something was wrong. I could have made her rest more.'

John's laugh was more like a strangled sob.

'Catch anyone making Liz do anything if she hadn't a mind to! That's why I could never persuade her to tell you . . .' He stopped, then: 'But this isn't the time or the place.'

Curiosity made Noelle glance at her uncle, compassion made her look away again. No, this wasn't the time to press him to complete his unfinished remark, and in fact several days elapsed before he returned to the subject of his own accord, days in which they had left the small town where Liz Madox-Browne had been born and now rested, and had returned to London. Noelle had completely forgotten his enigmatic words, until one morning, after breakfast, John called her into his study.

She wondered a little at the formality with which he invested the occasion. Normally, family affairs were discussed without ceremony across the meal table, the study being reserved for business matters only. Her uncle seemed ill at ease, she thought, and for a swift, panicky moment she wondered if he too were ill. His words did nothing to dispel that fear.

'It's taken me a while to pluck up my courage to tell you this, but I can't go on postponing it indefinitely.'

Noelle sat down rather suddenly in the chair he indicated, slender hands clasped anxiously in her lap.

'What is it, Uncle John? What's wrong?'

His agitation was further revealed by the way in which his large, capable hands disturbed the normally orderly thatch of greying hair.

'I hope,' he said bluntly, 'that you'll go on calling me "Uncle" even though we're not related in that way.'

'Not?' Noelle began, then relaxed. 'Well, only by marriage.'

John gave a sigh of pure desperation, his hands now engaged in systematically destroying a piece of paper.

'I'm no damned good at this kind of thing. I

wanted Liz to tell you herself, years ago, but she wouldn't. She was afraid of losing your respect.'

'Uncle?' Noelle tried to make a joke of the subject, to allay her own fears and what now seemed like his embarrassment. 'Are you trying to tell me after all this time that you two were never married?'

'I could wish it were that easy,' he told her grimly. 'No, Liz and I were legally husband and wife. What I'm trying to say, in my clumsy way, is that, rather than being your uncle, I could better claim to be your stepfather.'

'What?'

Noelle's vivacious little face paled, as she wondered for a moment if she were dreaming this, would waken to find it had been an incident forged in nightmare. She had lived with her aunt and uncle all her life, unable to remember her parents—relatives of her aunt, she had been told.

'Liz wasn't your aunt. She was your mother.' John continued to fiddle with the objects on his desk, as though unwilling to look at her drawn, incredulous features. 'You were born before I met and married her.'

'You mean I'm illegitimate? That is what you're trying to tell me?' Noelle's voice cracked.

'Yes—no, damn it!' He struck his hand on the desk. 'Oh, Liz wasn't married to your father, but I'm not telling you for that reason, but because I feel you're entitled to know your heritage, because circumstances have arisen . . .'

Unable to sit still a moment longer, Noelle got up and began to pace the large room.

'Why?' she demanded in a strangled voice. 'Why

didn't she tell me before? Didn't she realise what it would have meant to me to have a real mother? That I'd rather it'd been her than anyone else in the world?'

'My dear child!' John Madox-Browne sounded deeply moved, as he rose from his chair and joined her in the window embrasure. 'I'm so glad you feel that way. I felt sure you would, but I couldn't persuade her.'

She turned into the circle of his arm.

'I—I'm glad you told me, even though it's too late to be able to show her how much I—how much . . .' Her voice broke and she closed her eyes, bit hard on her lower lip. After a while she was able to continue. 'Why have you told me this now? Did she ask you to?'

'No,' John said gravely. 'Liz would have preferred the secret to be buried with her. She was deeply ashamed, you know. I had the devil's own job to persuade her to marry me all those years ago. I'm afraid your father left her with very deep scars, perhaps that never really healed, in spite of her love for me.'

'Did—do you think she loved my father?'

'I'm sure of it, my dear. Liz wasn't a woman to bestow herself lightly. But it's my opinion he wasn't worthy of her love, the damned rogue.'

'You know who he was?'

'Yes. He kept in touch, through his solicitors. He offered to pay Liz maintenance for you, but she refused to touch his money. He even,' John's voice rose in indignation, 'offered to adopt you.'

'So he knew about me, then?'

'He did!' John's mouth was still twisted in anger, 'and now Liz is—gone, he wants to meet you.'

'Hard luck!' was Noelle's instant reaction, 'because I certainly don't want to meet him!'

'I hoped you'd feel that way.' John spoke with relief, with satisfaction now. 'Then that's the end of the matter. I'll answer his letter, decline his invitation on your behalf.'

'You've had a letter from him? May I—may I see it?'

Rather reluctantly, she thought, John took a sheet of thick notepaper from the drawer in his desk and handed it to her. The cream paper was expensive, deckle-edged, the address gold-embossed below a crest of two hands clasping a heart.

'Claddagh Hall, by Lough Corrib, County Galway,' Noelle read aloud. She looked up at John for confirmation. 'My father's Irish?' At his brief nod, she read on. The letter was brief, the handwriting stark, blackly vigorous, demanding a visit from his natural daughter, 'to brighten my declining years'.

'Declining years, indeed!' John Madox-Browne snorted. 'Chap's a vigorous fifty-five at the most.'

The letter was signed simply 'Lissadell'.

'Is that his surname or his Christian name?' asked Noelle.

'Neither,' John said shortly, 'Noel O'Rourke, *Lord* Lissadell.'

'A lord?' Noelle said wonderingly.

'Yes, but don't let the fact impress you. A title is a pretty empty thing without the money to back it up.' John, a wealthy industrialist, himself in line for a title in the not too distant future, was in a position to know, she supposed.

'And my mother named me for him,' she mused. Despite her earlier decided affirmation, curiosity was taking hold of her and she found herself wondering if she resembled her father at all. Certainly she was nothing like her fair-haired, brown-eyed mother.

John didn't answer. There was no need, but he was watching her intently.

'Not having second thoughts, are you?' he hazarded shrewdly. 'Because if you are, I must warn you . . .'

'No—no—at least—well, I *am* curious,' she admitted. 'After all, it's not surprising, is it? I——'

'No,' he said heavily, 'not surprising, a feminine failing, that's all.' He returned to sit at his desk, and after a moment Noelle reseated herself, thoughtfully turning her father's letter over and over in her fingers.

'What are you thinking?' John probed, and she faced him frankly.

'That if I ignore this,' she indicated the letter, 'or let you refuse for me, I might regret it. Oh, not immediately, but in years to come, when it's too late. The way,' her voice wavered momentarily, 'the way it's too late now to tell my mother . . .'

'I understand,' John sighed. 'You may look like your father's family, but there's a lot of Liz in you and her besetting sin was curiosity. So?' He let the question hang in the air.

'I think,' slowly, 'that I *must* go to Ireland, just for a few days, that's all, just to see for myself, find my roots, I suppose.' Her blue eyes pleaded with him for understanding.

'And the business?'

At twenty-five, Noelle was already a successful fashion designer, and many well-known and titled customers patronised Noelle et Cie.

'Rachel and Manny can cope quite adequately for a while. Besides, I'm overdue for some kind of holiday.'

'You'll find the west of Ireland rather different from the South of France,' John commented drily, referring to her usual holiday location.

'Hmm, maybe! But even continuous sunshine tends to pall occasionally. Perhaps rain would make a nice change. It *does* rain a lot in Ireland, doesn't it?'

It was certainly raining that April morning, a few days later, when the Aer Lingus plane touched down at Dublin's airport, and it continued to rain as Noelle drove the hired car away from the airport and out into the green, fresh countryside. Impulsively she had decided to travel this way, in order to see as much as possible of her heritage, or half-heritage, she thought wryly.

Rachel and Manny Cohen, her partners and fellow designers, had raised no objection to her sudden departure, and when she had confided the reason for her visit, had not been so overwhelmed by its intriguing possibilities as to forget business.

'Keep your eyes open for some of those lovely Irish tweeds and that hand-made lace,' they adjured her.

The sun broke through for a while, as she took the

road from Dublin to Galway, along the Esker
Riada, the ridge of gravel hills which, for centuries,
had afforded travellers safe passage across the bog-
strewn central bowl of Ireland, through Kildare and
West Meath, to where the River Shannon marked
the boundary to Galway in Connacht.

Now the route followed meandering, minor
roads, alongside which the secret life of Ireland
continued undisturbed. Black and red cows chewed
by the wayside, while nearby lay farmsteads
cluttered with old pieces of machinery. Clucking
hens roosted on hay carts, and sheepdogs appeared
from nowhere to chase her car. She had broken her
journey overnight and as she continued on her way
next morning, Noelle realised she had no sense of
strangeness, of being an alien visitor. Was it, she
wondered fancifully, because she was half-Irish that
this pleasant land, its green threaded through with
grey, giving it a speckled look like a length of tweed
cloth, seemed to welcome her?

Within sight of Lough Corrib, she came suddenly
upon the house she sought. Claddagh Hall, a stone-
built mansion, stood on a grassy knoll, with wide
views across the lough to a mountain backdrop.
Green-backed islands, heightened by trees, dim-
pled the blue-black waters. On either side of a weed-
filled gravel drive, exotic flowering shrubs, untend-
ed, grew rampant, swamping the air with their
heady bouquet. The Hall would be a comfortless
place in winter, Noelle guessed as she halted the
car, the better to study her surroundings. The grey
stone walls would be stark protection against the
winter winds. Yet a strange thrill pierced her heart

as she stared at the building—the house of her ancestors, she romanced.

She gave herself a little shake. Not much use sitting here like a wide-eyed tourist. She must summon up the courage to present herself at the front door and ask to see her father.

A dour-faced manservant answered the door knocker's stiff, unwieldy summons and led her through the dark hall hung with staghorns, and into what appeared to be the dining room, with heavy, old-fashioned furnishings.

'I'll be telling Miss O'Rourke you're here.'

'*Miss* O'Rourke?'

'Himself's aunt.'

Her father must be out. Of course, Noelle reflected, he would be busy with estate affairs. She occupied her waiting time with studying the room. The O'Rourkes appeared to have a strong predilection for hunting, and by the same token they were decidedly not house-proud. Old hunting prints that must once have been colourful, now faded, adorned the walls, and a fox's mask was mounted above the fireplace, together with a dusty display of riding crops. The prevalent impression was one of dust-covered surfaces and decayed grandeur.

A sudden sensation that she was no longer alone made her turn, to encounter the scrutiny of a keen pair of eyes, set in a gentle, faded face.

'You must be Miss O'Rourke?' she asked. 'I'm Noelle Madox-Browne. My—my uncle,' she would never be able to think of John as anything else, 'my uncle had a letter from Lord Lissadell.'

'So *you're* Noel's daughter!' The old lady moved

forward with a briskness of which Noelle would not
have believed the tall, fragile frame capable. A soft
cheek was pressed to hers. '*Céad mile fáilte*, a
hundred thousand welcomes!' A hand on the girl's
arm, Miss O'Rourke steered her towards the
window. 'Yes!' It was a breath of satisfaction.
'You're very like him.'

'I suppose he's not available at the moment?'

Miss O'Rourke's face clouded over, its momen-
tary brightness replaced by regret.

'Didn't you know? You're too late, my dear,' and
at Noelle's look of dismay and dawning realisation,
'Oh, it's not your fault. Nobody could possibly have
foreseen it. He was fit and well, a man in the prime
of life. Such a stupid, unnecessary death.'

Noelle felt for the back of one of the hard-looking
chairs. No wonder the manservant had seemed
glum. Though she had never known her father, the
fact hit her that now she was doubly orphaned.

'How?' she began.

'The last hunt of the season. Noel was such a
dashing rider to hounds. Towards the end of the day
his horse stumbled and fell—tired, I suppose. The
horses always tired before Noel did, he was
indefatigable. He fell awkwardly. His—his neck
was broken.' Miss O'Rourke dabbed suddenly at
her eyes. 'Such a waste, and what's to become of us
all now I can't imagine.'

'Us?' Noelle enquired. 'I'm sorry, but I know
nothing about my—my father's family. I didn't
even know of his existence until a few days ago.'

'By "us", dear, I meant myself, the servants,
estate staff, stable-lads—and you, of course.'

'Me?'

'Yes, your father always meant to do something for you, I know.'

'Really, there's no need,' Noelle began.

'The moment he heard of your mother's death, he was determined. "Elizabeth can't keep the child from me now," he said.'

'Miss O'Rourke,' said Noelle firmly, 'let's get one thing quite straight. I didn't come here with any "expectations". I came because I was curious about my father, my background. I'm sorry I wasn't in time to meet him, but as it is I'll go straight back to England.'

'Oh, no! You'll stay a few days surely, for the funeral?' The old lady seemed to regard her anxiously and Noelle didn't see how she could refuse without appearing churlish and unfeeling. 'Your last respects,' Miss O'Rourke added persuasively.

Privately Noelle reflected that she had very little respect for the man who had fathered her and then allowed her mother to cope alone. Why hadn't he married Liz? She supposed she would never know now. It was one of the questions she had planned to ask him.

'You will stay?' Miss O'Rourke persisted, and slowly, reluctantly Noelle nodded. 'Oh, my dear, I'm so pleased. I would like the opportunity to get to know you. We've wondered so often ... But we must see about your room, and you'll take a cup of tea?' Noelle was to come to know this invitation well, for Miss O'Rourke drank tea at all times of the day, hot, sweet and strong. She pressed a bell by the fireplace. 'Sit yourself down. It will take Siobhan quite a while to get here. She's growing old, as are the rest of us, I'm afraid.'

'Tell me something about my father,' said Noelle, 'that is, if it's not too painful for you?'

The old lady nodded her head.

'Painful? Yes, but we mustn't be afraid to speak lovingly, reminiscently, of the dead. That's what keeps them alive for us, my dear Noelle. But where to begin? Such a complex man, a good man for all his faults, but a dreamer, an improvident! You'll have noticed the state of the house? All his time, all his spare money and energy was devoted to the upkeep of his stud.'

'He breeds—bred horses?'

'The love of his life, and there's many a fellow Irishman like him. It was his dream to breed a horse that would restore his fortunes, and if determination were enough he might have done it too, some day, my poor boy.'

'Had he any other children?' Noelle asked hesitantly. She didn't want her curiosity to sound as if she made any claim on Noel O'Rourke's estate, not that it sounded as if such a claim would be worth much. Rather, she longed to know if she had other relations.

'No, Lissadell's wife died childless, a year or two ago. It was the sorrow of their lives, and my younger nephew, Seamus, died abroad long ago and had no legitimate heirs either.'

'Then what happens to Claddagh Hall, the estate?'

'That depends upon the will.' Miss O'Rourke

spoke rather oddly, Noelle thought, but as nothing else was forthcoming, she forgot the incident.

The funeral was over. Noelle and Miss O'Rourke were the last of the mourners to leave the little churchyard where the last of the Lissadells was now buried amidst his ancestors. The small church of St Patrick had been filled to overflowing by estate workers, friends and acquaintances. Listening intently as Miss O'Rourke made a point of exchanging a few words, shaking every proffered hand, Noelle learnt just how popular her father had been, and although she had come to Ireland determined to be prejudiced against him for her mother's sake, now she found herself regretting, for her own sake, that she had never met him and heard the other side of a very incomplete story.

'You've never told me why Lord Lissadell didn't marry my mother,' she reminded Miss O'Rourke as the car carried them back to the Hall. Noel O'Rourke had been buried almost within sight of his home, but the driveway from church to hall was too much for his elderly aunt to walk.

'It's very simple, my dear, no mystery. I thought you might have known. Ours is a Catholic family and Noel was already married when he met and committed his "indiscretion" with your mother.'

'Where *was* that? Where did he meet her? I know so little.'

'In England. He had a promising horse; the poor dear boy always had a promising horse which didn't live up to expectations. It was running at Newmarket. He stayed at a public house in a nearby town,

Haverhill—I believe that's in Suffolk? Your mother was the landlord's daughter.'

There was no time for further conversation. As Noelle assisted Miss O'Rourke from the car and up the steps into the house, the manservant appeared and informed them that the 'lawyer's man' had come on ahead after the funeral and was awaiting them.

'He'll want to talk about the will.' Miss O'Rourke removed her hat with hands that trembled a little. 'Oh dear, I feel quite apprehensive.'

'Try not to worry,' Noelle urged her. 'I'm sure your nephew will have made provision for you, and if he hasn't we'll think of something.' In the few days since she had arrived at Claddagh Hall, she had become very attached to the gentle old lady, who was after all a blood relation, her great-aunt.

Miss O'Rourke patted her arm.

'Thank you, dear, but I've no intention of becoming a burden to you, or to anyone else. I do have a little money of my own. I'll get by, whatever happens.'

Mr Kelly, the elderly solicitor, was in a state of apologetic indignation.

'To be sure, Miss O'Rourke, 'tis altogether too bad of him, so it is.'

'Too bad of whom? Do compose yourself, man. Sit down and explain quietly.' No one would have believed that a moment ago she had been as agitated as he.

'Why, Fergus Carrick, to be sure. His Lordship's nephew. Didn't I spend months tracking him down all those years ago, when we learnt of his existence, hasn't he visited here freely ever since, and now when I telephone, long distance, mark you, and leave a message about his uncle's death, does he get in touch with me? Indeed he does not. Not a word I've heard, and me unable to read the will without him present.'

'Perhaps he didn't receive the message,' Miss O'Rourke suggested.

'And perhaps he did,' Mr Kelly said darkly. 'Wasn't there no love lost lately between him and His Lordship. Every time he was here, weren't there rows and arguments?'

'To be fair,' Miss O'Rourke was at her most judicial, 'that was partly Lissadell's fault, his ridiculous prejudice against Fergus's father. He never felt Richard Carrick was good enough for my niece, his sister. And Noel could be intensely irritating with his feckless ways. Dear Fergus is so methodical.'

'Be that as it may,' Mr Kelly was not to be placated, 'I've a will to be read and no one to be reading it to. So if you'll excuse me, Miss O'Rourke, I'll be off back to Dublin. I'm a busy man. Perhaps you'll be letting me know if you hear anything of Mr Fergus Carrick?'

'I really ought to go home, Aunt Bridie,' Noelle told Miss O'Rourke a few days later. The elderly woman had insisted on the less formal mode of address.

'And I thought you were enjoying your visit, that you liked Claddagh,' Bridie O'Rourke said reproachfully.

'I am—I do. I love Claddagh Hall. I love Ireland,

and most of all I love you. But I've no business being here. I ought to go before this Fergus Carrick turns up, or he might get the wrong idea.'

'We'll worry about that when we hear he's on his way. Do stay a little longer,' Miss O'Rourke pleaded persuasively. 'It's so nice to have feminine company for a change, and Claddagh would be very lonely without you now.'

And so Noelle allowed herself to be persuaded, a decision she was soon to regret.

Up early one morning, she wandered into the dining room where Miss O'Rourke had received her and noticing, not for the first time, the coat of dust that obscured the beautiful surface of the long refectory-type table, she felt a sudden compulsion to restore it to its rightful glory. It seemed a shame to her that the house had been allowed to fall into such a state of neglect, but, as Bridie had pointed out, the household staff were sadly under-strength and those remaining were growing old.

Five minutes later, armed with cloths and wax polish purloined from old Siobhan's domain, she was vigorously engaged on her task, when she heard a brisk, impatient step on the tiled floor of the hall. On fine days the great front door was left wide open, and someone had taken advantage of its invitation.

That someone was a man, awesomely tall in appearance to the diminutive Noelle. He was lean and rangily built with a hawk-like face, the fleshless angles of cheek and jaw-bone softened by a beard, greyer—with an almost reddish tinge—than the variegated mane of sable and silver that grew overlong at neck and brow. His impatient glance fell upon Noelle as she stood, polishing implements in hand.

'Where's your mistress, girl? I see the place is still left open to the four winds, no sense of security.'

At his words Noelle stiffened. The visitor had obviously mistaken her for a maidservant, and while she couldn't blame him—her occupation and her casual blouse and skirt covered by one of Siobhan's voluminous aprons were misleading—she did resent his tone. Servants were as much entitled to courtesy as their employers.

'Miss O'Rourke isn't up yet,' she began, 'and I'm . . .'

'Be so good as to tell her I'm here, and hurry up about it, girl. Don't stand there staring at me! Are you new here or something?'

Noelle's sense of humour was never far from the surface, whatever the occasion. This top-lofty man with his arrogant demeanour took her for a servant. She would enjoy seeing his expression when he discovered her to be a member of the family. She restrained an impish impulse to bob him a curtsey, but asked in a suitably demure manner:

'Who shall I say has called, sir?'

His eyes narrowed and he observed her more closely.

'You're English.'

'Yes, sir.'

'Hmm.' He dismissed the unimportant fact with a grunt. 'Well, whatever your name is, kindly tell Miss O'Rourke that Fergus Carrick, her great-nephew, is here.'

Just in time Noelle managed to mask her

astonishment. So this was, what, her cousin? She supposed that loosely described their relationship.

Her survey of him became more comprehensive, as she noted the austere expression, his gipsyish tan. In fact there was something altogether gipsyish about his whole appearance, the casual clothes, slacks and tweed jacket, with a scarf instead of a tie carelessly knotted at his throat, and the wild, almost Bohemian hair and beard.

'Be able to describe me in detail, will you,' he asked with heavy irony, 'just in case I steal the spoons while your back's turned. Hurry up, girl, for goodness' sake! Enough time's been wasted already.'

'By you!' retorted Noelle, forgetting for a moment the role allotted to her and which she had decided to play. 'Even if I call Miss O'Rourke this very minute, you won't get to hear the contents of your uncle's will today. Solicitors don't hang about and Mr Kelly's gone back to Dublin.'

'Don't be so damned impertinent!' Fergus Carrick roared. 'My God, my uncle was pretty come-day-go-day in his arrangements, but surely even he didn't put up with this kind of back-chat?'

'I couldn't say, I'm sure, sir.' Noelle slipped back into role and sidled from the room, settling for discretion. But Fergus Carrick wouldn't have to wait long for his come-uppance!

She found Bridie O'Rourke dressing and swiftly put her in the picture, omitting her own clash with Fergus.

'Oh dear, now we shall be all set at odds,' Miss O'Rourke sighed. 'Fergus is a dear, but such a restless creature. You'll come down with me, Noelle. I'd like you to meet him.'

'I wouldn't miss it for the world,' Noelle said truthfully, 'but I'll just tidy myself up a little.'

Thankful for the providence which had prompted her to pack a decent selection from her wardrobe at home, she selected a dress with which to replace the blouse and skirt. A simple day dress, its very simplicity was deceptive. One of Noelle's own designs, its cut was every inch *haute couture*, its lines clinging flatteringly to her slight but shapely figure, the blue of the material echoing that of her eyes. She allowed her dark hair, which had been tied back, to swing loosely about her face and shoulders.

About to leave her room once more, she paused thoughtfully, eyeing her reflection in the long mirror. Why did she feel impelled to take so much trouble over her appearance? Was it just because Fergus Carrick had taken her for a maid, accorded her no more interest than he would have done had she been a servant? That was partly so. But there was more to it.

It hadn't been only the suddenness, the unexpectedness of Fergus's arrival that had startled her, quickened her pulse-rate. It had been the even more unsettling effect upon her of his undeniably romantic appearance, and, more than just his looks, the aura of masculinity he projected, bringing into the room a presence which seemed subtly to alter its quiet atmosphere to one of enlivening excitement and challenge.

Yes, Noelle was looking forward for more reasons than one to her next encounter with Fergus Carrick.

CHAPTER TWO

FOLLOWING demurely in Miss O'Rourke's necessarily slow and dignified wake, Noelle was conscious of an increasing tendency to breathlessness. She could well understand her great-aunt's apprehension about the turmoil that would attend Fergus's arrival at Claddagh Hall. She was all too aware on her own account of his disturbing propensities.

'Fergus!' Miss O'Rourke moved towards him with outstretched hands, any misgivings she might have concealed by an undoubtedly affectionate welcome. 'It's good to see you again.'

'And you, Aunt Bridie!' Tall as Miss O'Rourke was, Fergus had to bend to take her in his arms. 'And not a day older than when I last saw you!' Fergus Carrick, like Noelle, might be only half Irish, she reflected, but there was no doubt he had inherited the kiss of the Blarney Stone. 'I'm sorry I wasn't here for the funeral. I only found Kelly's message yesterday, when I got back from Paris. I set out again straight away.'

'Fergus, I want you meet your cousin, Noelle Madox-Browne.' Miss O'Rourke drew her forward. 'Noel's daughter.'

Noelle found herself subjected to a very comprehensive survey by a pair of deep-set, velour-brown eyes.

'I see!' he said; that was all, but Noelle felt that he

did indeed see, a lot. He had heard of her existence, that was very evident, and although Noelle had firmly decided that the erring ways of her parent were no reflection on her, she felt herself colouring uncomfortably. But her stead gaze refused to drop before his.

To say that Fergus was astonished by Noelle's presence was, he felt, to put it mildly. What had brought the girl here? Acquisitiveness? She didn't look the hard, mercenary type, but you never could tell. Still, if she was expecting rich pickings here, she was in for a shock.

He found himself prey to a whole host of emotions. Not normally an irascible man, he regretted the unfortunate tone of their first encounter, his nerves exacerbated by travelling delays and the sudden loss of his uncle, of whom, despite his faults, he had been excessively fond. The error he had made in mistaking Noelle for a servant he discounted as being no fault of his own, yet, inexplicably, it still angered him. Why hadn't she enlightened him as to her identity, instead of going through with her ridiculous charade? Perhaps she had felt unable to face him, unsupported, with the truth? Perhaps she was ashamed? No, she wasn't ashamed. Those clear blue Irish eyes, so damnably like Lissadell's, were frank and clear, her freckled, vivacious little face serene with perhaps just the slightest suspicion of provocation in the curl of her mouth. Damn it, was she daring to laugh at him?

He made his expression deliberately cool and insolent as he looked her over. She was daintily built, he noted approvingly. He abhorred voluptuous females. Boy-slim, but feminine withal. A sight too much character in her face to warrant the description of 'pretty'. Arresting would be more accurate, and he was willing to bet that that firmly modelled, pointed jaw hinted at obstinacy. He felt the tingling spice of challenge run through his veins. Such a little slip of a thing, but spunky, he felt certain. How would she respond to provocation? he wondered humorously. The brown eyes narrowed into a deliberately speculative line and he allowed his mouth to twist into sardonic wryness.

'Ah yes,' he drawled, 'Lissadell's "misdemeanour".'

Noelle went rigid. She had steeled herself to endure his seemingly endless scrutiny, making good use of the time for her own appraisal, noting the high-bridged, chiselled nose, the well shaped lips, the dark, determined lines of his brows, but she hadn't been prepared for such forthright insolence.

'Mr Carrick,' she said icily, 'if you must be rude, why not be honestly so? I can assure you polite euphemisms are quite unnecessary. Yes, I *am* Lissadell's "bastard daughter", but you can scarcely hold me to blame for that fact.'

'My dear Noelle!' Miss O'Rourke gasped. 'Fergus, really! What a way to greet each other!'

The straightness of Fergus Carrick's face hid the belying twinkle in his eyes.

'My apologies to you, Aunt Bridie, but don't you find it singularly curious that Noel's daughter, after ignoring his existence all her life, should descend upon us so immediately after his death? It makes me ask myself what she hopes to gain.'

'Nothing!' snapped Noelle before Miss O'Rourke could reply. 'For your information, the facts are that I didn't know of my father's existence until just over a week ago and, until I got here, I didn't know he was dead.'

'But then we only have your word for both "facts",' Fergus drawled.

How could she have thought this man attractive, to the point where she had been anxious to appear at her best before him? Disdaining to answer his latest taunt, Noelle turned to Miss O'Rourke.

'Aunt Bridie, I think the time has come for me to go home. I've enjoyed my visit and meeting you, but I don't see any prospect of further enjoyment, now.' A scornful sideways glance from the blue eyes made it quite clear who was the author of her doubt.

'Noelle!' Miss O'Rourke was distressed. 'My dear, don't do anything hasty. Fergus, tell her you didn't mean . . .'

'Oh, but I did, Aunt, I did, and Miss Browne's reactions only confirm my suspicions.' Just how far would that streak of pride take her?

Noelle's pointed chin was very much in evidence as she turned to stalk from the room.

'I'll see you before I leave, Aunt Bridie, when you're *alone*.'

In her room she threw things into a suitcase, with a fine disregard for orderliness. She couldn't wait to get away from Claddagh Hall, or, more correctly, away from Fergus Carrick. It was apparent that he was, or expected to be, Noel O'Rourke's heir and that he resented what he saw as her attempt to poach on his preserves. But despite her haste to quit the Hall, she felt a pang of real regret. In the few days she had been there, the house, and Ireland itself, soft and beautiful, the people she had met warm and friendly, had laid strong claim to her heart, and in that sense she would be sorry to leave.

As she descended the main staircase, she could still hear voices raised in argument coming from the dining room and she hesitated. It would be impolite, unkind, to leave without making her farewells to Bridie, but she didn't want to run the gamut of those mocking brown eyes again, those ironic, gipsyish features with their odd attraction. She admitted to cowardice. She was afraid that if she saw him again it would be all the harder to erase his image from her mind. It was intensely annoying to find herself so fascinated, so captivated by mere outward essentials, when the man himself was a despicable boor.

Then, as the volume of one of the voices rose slightly, the words awfully clear to the indignant hearer, her decision was made. 'And of course, as is usual when there's a death, the vultures gather, eh, Auntie?'

This was intolerable. She would write to Bridie when she got home. The older woman would surely sympathise with her distaste for facing the instigator of such an insult. Thankful that the heavy door, which had a tendency to groan alarmingly, was still open, Noelle left the building and hurried around the side of the house to the stableyard, where her car was parked. She would have liked to take a final farewell of the horses, whose beautiful, intelligent faces looked out over the half doors, but if she were to be away before Miss O'Rourke noticed her absence, there was no time to linger.

Rounding the car to reach the driver's side, Noelle froze. Lying in its shade were two grey, shaggy shapes, that looked enormous to her fear-widened eyes. Where had these beasts come from? She hadn't encountered any dogs at Claddagh before. An incident with an unruly Alsation when she was three years old had left Noelle with a terror of dogs, particularly large ones, which she had vainly tried to overcome. Now, with her eyes fixed on their enquiring uplifted heads, she backed away. She would use the passenger door and slide across behind the wheel.

To her horror the animals showed a distinct interest in her actions and one of them rose, strolling leisurely towards her, its tail a gentle pendulum. Noelle's horror intensified. The creature was larger even than she had imagined, its head almost on a level with her chin, and its mate, who had joined in the investigation, followed a few steps behind.

With a sudden burst of enthusiastic activity, the leading wolfhound bounded towards her and, rearing up, placed a paw on either of Noelle's shoulders, its face enquiringly close to hers, its open mouth and lolling tongue revealing enormous white teeth. With a shriek, she let fall her suitcase and continued to scream, not hearing the sound of pounding footsteps.

'Down, Caesar! Cleo, sit!' A pair of hands descended on the shoulders where the large shaggy paws had rested and Noelle found herself being shaken vigorously. 'For God's sake, girl, shut up! Anyone would think you were being eaten alive!'

In spite of her fear, Noelle managed a flash of spirit.

'For all I know I might have been, if you——'

'Nonsense! Cleo and Caesar are the gentlest of creatures.' Then the scornful brown eyes had spotted the suitcase. 'And what are you up to?'

'Leaving,' she retorted, 'which should please you. Claddagh Hall isn't big enough to hold both of us.'

He chose to misinterpret her words.

'No? I suppose you were hoping to have it all to yourself? Hard luck, Miss Browne, but you'll agree that my claim is more "legitimate" than yours?'

How dared he taunt her with that word, pointing up the invidious circumstances of her birth? Hateful man!

'For your information, my name is *Madox-Browne*, and if you'll keep those two brutes of yours at bay, I'll relieve you of my presence.'

'Oh, no!' He picked up the suitcase, with every appearance of not intending to relinquish it. 'You're not going anywhere.' Did he think she had the family silver in there?

'You wouldn't be thinking of searching my belongings first?' she enquired coldly. She wouldn't put it past him.

'Oh, I don't think that will be necessary, do you? It must be apparent even to you by now that Noel's idea of material possessions only extended to the finest horseflesh money could buy.' He nodded towards the stables, where the more valuable of the

Lissadell stud were housed alongside a pair of magnificent hunters.

'Then would you kindly hand me my case and allow me to be on my way? I've a long drive ahead of me.'

'No,' he said, and before she could part her lips in indignant protest, 'no, you can't have your case, and no you're not leaving, yet. For some reason, best known to herself, my good aunt wants you to stay. Apparently she finds your presence essential to her wellbeing. I'm extremely fond of my aunt, therefore you're staying.'

'But I . . .' She wasn't allowed to proceed. A strong tanned hand had hold of her elbow, propelling her back towards the front of the house, and Noelle knew that however hard she struggled she would be no match for his tensile strength. Dignity was all she had left to her.

They found Miss O'Rourke hovering anxiously on the steps.

'Then it was *you* who screamed, my dear? What is it? Are you hurt?'

'Not a scratch, Auntie,' her nephew informed her cheerfully, before Noelle could answer. 'It would appear Noel's daughter doesn't share his love for four-footed creatures.'

'That's not true!' Noelle snapped. 'I love horses. It's just dogs.' She couldn't repress a shudder.

Miss O'Rourke's face cleared, but then she caught sight of the suitcase Fergus still held.

'You weren't leaving us?' she said reproachfully. 'Without a word of goodbye.'

'She *was*,' Fergus said succinctly, 'but she isn't

now, are you, Miss *Madox*—Browne? For my aunt's sake, you've agreed to stay.' His brown eyes dared her to contradict.

Noelle mumbled something incoherent. Her thoughts were in a turmoil. Wounded pride, common sense, told her she ought to leave, but— and it wasn't only consideration for Bridie O'Rourke's feelings that made her waver, it was the galvanic touch of those strong fingers still gripping her arm, the tingling warmth they imparted to her flesh. Unpleasant as Fergus Carrick had been, the conflict with him had made her feel more vitally alive than she had since the depression following Liz's death and the revelation of their true relationship. And in spite of Fergus's hostility, her own anger, and his unjustifiable suspicions, she still felt strangely drawn to him. There was a challenge to be found in altering his attitude towards her, and a challenge was something Noelle could never resist.

'Maybe I will stay a few more days,' she spoke to Bridie, ignoring Fergus, 'if *you* really want me to?'

'Indeed I do, dear,' Miss O'Rourke said fervently, moving back into the house, 'and now, let's order breakfast and converse in a civilised manner.'

'Why not?' Fergus agreed smoothly. 'Perhaps we could discuss the terms of Miss Browne's stay here. Incidentally, I refuse to keep uttering that ridiculous double-barrelled mouthful.'

'Terms?' Noelle enquired suspiciously.

'Naturally!' He sounded surprised that she should find it necessary to ask. 'If your motives are as altruistic as you claim, you surely won't wish to be dependent on charity? For I assume you *are* hard up, or you wouldn't be here hoping for a handout. I'm sure we can find some gainful employment for you. Perhaps,' his mouth curled fleetingly, a movement that might have been attractive but for the mockery implied, 'perhaps as a housemaid, since your talents seem to lie in that direction?'

'Fergus!' Miss O'Rourke spoke repressively. 'That will do! Noelle, take no notice. He has a somewhat warped sense of humour. You'll remain here as *my* guest. These suspicions are unworthy of you, Fergus. Dear Noelle came here purely out of filial loyalty and remained at my suggestion, not her own.'

'The filial loyalty I beg leave to doubt,' Fergus murmured, 'but as you wish, Aunt, as you wish.'

'That man!' stormed Noelle as Fergus, having declined breakfast, left her with Miss O'Rourke. 'He makes my blood boil!'

'But not your heart beat faster, dear?' the older woman asked with a mischievous twinkle. 'He's very good-looking, you'll agree, and most disarming when he's in a good mood, though *so* restless, just like his dear mother.'

'Handsome is as handsome does,' Noelle quoted. 'Personally I find him totally lacking in attraction, though perhaps a haircut and shave might improve him. And how dare he refer to me as "a vulture"?'

'Vulture, dear?' Miss O'Rourke looked mystified, then, 'Oh, I see, you overheard. My dear, he was talking about the tradesmen. All pressing for their bills to be paid. Noel was always behindhand.'

If Noelle was a trifle ashamed of her hasty assumption, she quelled the feeling. No doubt he had said far worse things about her that she hadn't overheard.

Later that day she was given striking evidence of what Miss O'Rourke had meant when she deplored Fergus's energetic nature. His inspection of house and estate had something of the effect of a whirlwind, and since it would have been too tiring for Miss O'Rourke to accompany him in his attic-to-cellar expedition, he insisted, for some reason Noelle couldn't fathom, that she do so.

'I've already seen over the house,' she protested.

'I'm sure you have,' was his satirical reply, 'but did you know what you were looking for, or recognise it if you found it? Just how good is your business acumen, Miss Browne?'

'For heaven's sake!' Noelle was becoming increasingly irritated by this truncated version of her surname. 'If it's too much trouble to give me my full name, call me Noelle.'

'Are you sure'—there was irony in the brown eyes—'that you want to be on such intimate terms with me?'

'No, I'm not sure,' she retorted, 'but since you're so odiously familiar and insulting in the way you talk to me——'

'Then "Noelle" it shall be. My name, as you know, is Fergus. Feel free to use it.'

Immediately she decided that if it could possibly be avoided, she would not address him as anything.

'What *are* we looking for?' Noelle demanded, as Fergus picked his way through rambling attics, crammed to overflowing with the accumulations of generations of O'Rourkes.

'Anything of possible value,' he said, brushing aside a layer of cobwebs that impeded his progress, and for the first time she noticed the ring he wore on the little finger of his right hand. A gold ring, its design was that of a heart clasped in two hands. The Lissadell crest, she thought with a spurt of indignation, and he wasn't even an O'Rourke. But he had noticed her silence and she said:

'Would anything valuable be stored up here?'

'Who knows?' he shrugged. 'The junk our grandparents and great-grandparents collected are the antique finds of today.'

'You're looking for things to sell!' she accused, and he shot her an ironic look.

'Well, naturally. You don't suppose I'll be able to manage the upkeep of this place out of my own resources?' He was so blithely certain Claddagh would be his, Noelle fumed. 'If we can't find anything,' he went on, 'the whole place may have to go under the hammer.'

'Oh, no!' she said involuntarily. 'How could you?'

'It's not what I want,' he told her, 'but it might be a case of necessity. If Lissadell's left money as well as the property, which incidentally I doubt, everything will be plain sailing. Otherwise . . .' He shrugged again.

'You can't be sure yet that he hasn't,' she argued.

'Knowing my uncle, it's almost a foregone conclusion.'

'You seem to be very sure Claddagh's going to be yours!' Noelle couldn't refrain from voicing her thoughts.

'Disappointed? Perhaps you thought it was going to be yours?'

'I thought nothing of the sort,' she replied with dignity. 'I'm not one of your "vultures".' She saw that he recognised the reference and for a brief instant amusement showed in his eyes.

Their preliminary survey of the attic yielded nothing of immediate interest, and Noelle, thinking furiously, followed Fergus down to the next floor. If she had stood to inherit Claddagh Hall, she knew she would have done everything in her power to keep house and estate in the family, so she couldn't really blame Fergus for seeking out items of possible commercial value. Maybe he wasn't in her happy position of having a prosperous business, and not only that, but a wealthy, indulgent 'uncle', who, having no children of his own, had also expressed his readiness to supply financial backing for any future project Noelle might undertake. If Claddagh were hers, she would restore it to its former magnificence.

'Nothing but a few dreary old family portraits, probably by some very inferior artist,' Fergus concluded, as they completed their tour of inspection, 'but then, of course, I'm no expert.'

'Besides, you couldn't sell *them*,' Noelle pointed out. 'Family portraits belong to the house.'

'Afraid ancient Lissadells might turn somersaults in their graves?'

'And if you sell up,' Noelle went on, ignoring this levity, 'what will happen to Aunt Bridie? This is her home.'

'I don't know.' Fergus's manner altered and he sounded a trifle weary. 'In any case, it's no good deciding anything until the will's been read. You never know, Lissadell might have decided to leave the lot to a retirement home for racehorses!'

Their tour of the estate did little to lighten Fergus's mood. Although, in direct contrast to the Hall, those parts of the grounds which related to stableyard and stud were impeccably maintained, it had not been without considerable expense, and the office attached to the stable block yielded up a bureau-full of unpaid bills for hay, feed and other similar expenses. Fergus stared at them bleakly.

'My God,' he groaned, 'what a mess!'

'Perhaps he just didn't have the opportunity to settle them before he died,' Noelle suggested hopefully. 'Perhaps there's money in the bank to——'

He shook his head.

'Unlikely. Lissadell was notorious for being in arrears. The next year's bills would have been in before he'd paid these. My uncle was a charming man, but almost childishly naïve. It was always a case of "something will turn up". There was always a promising filly or colt that would do well some day, and some day was usually never. If the animal lived up to its promise physically, invariably it would break a leg or its neck. How anyone could bear to live in such a hand-to-mouth fashion, I can't imagine.'

'You being totally practical and businesslike, I suppose?' Noelle asked sarcastically, remembering Bridie's remark that he was 'methodical'. What right had he, though, to criticise Noel O'Rourke, when by his own admission he himself didn't amount to much financially?

'As it happens, yes. I race in a small way myself, but I cut my coat according to my cloth and if I can't afford to pay for something, then I wait until I can.'

'I see!' she said provocatively. 'You starve *your* horses then?'

'I wasn't referring to essentials, but to the horses themselves. Lissadell had only to hear of a likely animal, be it at home or in England, and he must be buying it.'

'And do you breed horses as well?'

'Yes.' Suddenly a quick, eloquent smile lit his face, altering its expression to a startling degree. 'You see, I haven't altogether escaped my Irish heritage.'

The words themselves went almost unheeded, as Noelle marvelled at the incredible way the smile enhanced his appearance. If his features were always so pleasantly irradiated, he would be even more devastating to her newly discovered susceptibilities, but, perhaps fortunately, the smile was short-lived.

'If this place had been in better shape, I might have been prepared to sell up my own farm and stud and move in. But I don't see how——'

'In that case,' Noelle interrupted—she was feeling strangely tense and edgy—'let's hope it *has* been left to retired racehorses!'

It was a day or two more before they were to learn the fate of Claddagh, when Mr Kelly returned from

Dublin. At Miss O'Rourke's insistence, Noelle was present at the reading of the will, though she had protested vehemently against her inclusion.

'It doesn't concern me. Fergus won't like it.'

And certainly the brown eyes had narrowed searchingly when she followed Bridie into the dining room, but with Mr Kelly present he could make no comment.

Theirs was a small gathering at the long table, which could easily have seated twenty, its surface gleaming with Noelle's continued attentions. For want of better occupation, she had turned her energies to the housework and, perhaps encouraged by her example, the small household staff had set to work with a will so that although still undeniably shabby, Claddagh Hall had taken on some of the gleam of its palmier days.

'Fergus, lad, what delayed you at all?' and without waiting for an answer, 'It's glad I am to see you still here, Miss Madox-Browne,' Mr Kelly declared as he spread his papers before him, though Noelle knew it must be a mere expression of courtesy. 'Because,' he continued, dumbfounding her, 'hasn't His Lordship expressly mentioned you in his will?'

'He has?' Noelle dared not turn her head to encounter Fergus's gaze, but kept her eyes fixed on the elderly solicitor.

'Yes, indeed. Wait a while till I tell you. There's divil a penny, as maybe you'll have guessed for yourselves, but what there is, the Hall and the stud, is left jointly between you and young Fergus here,' he paused, 'on the condition that you both live here, keep the Hall and its lands a going proposition, and that the pair of you make a home for Miss O'Rourke.'

'What?' This was Fergus.

'Impossible!' Noelle said. Though a discreet telephone call while Fergus and Bridie O'Rourke were out of the way had assured her that her business was running smoothly, that Rachel and Manny could well manage without her for a while longer, she knew she must soon return to London. Apart from her responsibilities to her partners and their clients, it wasn't in her nature to be idle for long.

Mr Kelly looked from one to the other.

''Tis your decision, of course, but if either of you refuses to comply with the terms of the will, everything is to be sold and——'

'Sent to a retirement home for racehorses?' Fergus cut in ironically, and Noelle stared at him. How could he joke about it?

Mr Kelly, too, looked taken aback.

'No, sir, no, to be sure. But yourself already being a gentleman of property, so to speak, the money from the sale would go to Miss Madox-Browne.'

'What?' Noelle couldn't have been more horri-fied if the money *had* been going to some charity.

'I see!' Fergus spoke in that exasperating drawl which so annoyed her. 'So either way, Miss Browne is not to be the loser?'

'Indeed not, sir.' Mr Kelly took the remark at face value, sounding shocked at the suggestion that it should be otherwise. 'All his life His Lordship felt some recompense was due to his daughter, particularly as her mother steadfastly refused his offers of assistance.'

There was a long silence.

'I won't accept it,' Noelle said abruptly. 'I don't need it. I'm well able to support myself.' She glared defiantly at Fergus, saw the heavy black bar of his brows rise incredulously. 'Don't look at me in that insufferably insolent fashion!' she snapped. 'I mean it. I'm twenty-five and for the last six years I've lived on what I could earn.'

It was true. Once her salary as a trainee designer had been sufficient to support her, she had refused to accept any further allowance from the Madox-Brownes and latterly Noelle et Cie had prospered to the extent that she was a young woman of some means, though that was none of Fergus Carrick's business.

'So I'll be giving you a day or so to discuss it,' Mr Kelly announced, and refused to hear of any hasty decision being made. Thus Miss O'Rourke saw the lawyer out and the beneficiaries of the will faced each other across the table.

'It would seem,' Fergus said, 'that we're stuck with each other.' His choice of words was intensely annoying.

'We most certainly are not!' Noelle retorted. 'There's no way I'll agree to share a house with you.'

'But what if I'm equally determined the sale price of Claddagh shan't fall into your sticky little hands?'

'I told you,' Noelle said savagely, 'I don't want the money.'

'How can you avoid it otherwise? You heard the terms of the will?'

'There must be some way round it!'

'Only one. We both move in and try to put the place back on its feet.'

'Or you could buy me out,' she suggested.

'Impossible! Can't afford it. We'll just have to put up with each other.'

Noelle parted her lips to protest further, then closed them and became thoughtful. True, her first reaction to the terms of the will had been a determination to steer clear of any situation that involved Fergus Carrick, to remove herself as soon as possible from the sphere of his disturbing influence. Apart from his resentment of her presence, she was afraid that, in any prolonged association with him, she might not be able to conceal the humiliating truth, that he troubled her peace of mind as no other man had been able to on such short acquaintance. On the other hand, she didn't want to be accused of acquisitiveness, a charge he would certainly level against her if Claddagh Hall had to be sold.

But two far stronger considerations motivated her change of heart: the genuine affection she had come to feel for Bridie O'Rourke and, incredibly romantic folly, that she had fallen in love at first sight, a devotion that only a lifetime's servitude could fulfil, with Claddagh Hall itself. Her inward communing with herself concluded, she met Fergus's ironic gaze with a defiant tilt of her head.

'All right! We'll do it, but only,' she added hastily, 'for the sake of the Hall and Aunt Bridie.'

'Of course! Although we might even go further,' he said slowly, and as her eyes questioned him, 'the most obvious solution to all this is for us to get married. Then our interests would be mutual.'

The crazy, startled gymnastics her heart was performing made Noelle slow in replying, but when she did, her voice was cold with the knowledge that he was mocking her and she didn't find it amusing.

'Ours will be a purely *business* arrangement.'

CHAPTER THREE

'I ALMOST changed my mind again when he said that,' Noelle confessed afterwards to her great-aunt.

'It sounds a very sensible idea to me,' Bridie confounded her by saying. 'I must admit it's one that had occurred to me. You could do far worse. He'll make a good husband, a real rock to lean on, quite unlike poor Noel. Your father, my dear, was not always a reliable man. Yes, the more I think about it, the better I like the idea of you and Fergus together.'

Noelle was not unaware of Bridie's strong partiality for her great-nephew, but she wouldn't have suspected her of a tendency towards matchmaking.

'Forget it, Aunt Bridie,' she advised. 'Even if I were mad enough to agree, purely for the sake of Claddagh, it would be a total disaster. You must have noticed the effect we have on each other?'

'Hmmm!' was Bridie's only comment.

'I only agreed to stay on,' Noelle continued hastily, 'because I won't have him accusing me of being after the money. I really don't need it. You see . . .'

Her phone calls, home to John Madox-Browne, and to her office, had been received with dismayed incredulity. Both John and the Cohens had pleaded with her to reconsider.

'How you can even think of giving everything up, just to vegetate in a broken-down old house in Ireland,' Rachel Cohen wailed. 'You want to go mad? What will you do with yourself?'

'I shan't be giving it all up,' Noelle explained. 'I shall still design clothes for Noelle et Cie and I'll be backwards and forwards so often you'll scarcely notice I'm not there all the time.'

'But to plough so much of your hard-earned money into a place that only half belongs to you.'

'That,' said Noelle sharply, 'is top secret as far as Fergus is concerned. He's not to know that it's my money, which is why I want Manny to come over to Claddagh and say he's an art expert from one of the big London firms . . .'

'Manny? An expert? On art?' Rachel screamed with laughter. 'My Manny is a business man. What he knows about pictures you could write on your thumbnail.'

'He only has to pretend, for heaven's sake. I've dug some old oil paintings out of the attic. I just want Manny to rave about them. I'll tell him how much to offer . . .'

'Who is paying for these pictures?' Rachel asked suspiciously.

'I am,' Noelle laughed. 'All Manny has to do is take them away.'

'And what do you want he should do with them?'

'Oh, I don't know. Yes, I do. You can hang them in the salon.'

'This "cousin" of yours,' Rachel probed suspiciously, 'you haven't by any chance fallen for him?'

'Certainly not,' Noelle denied, too hastily, 'I can't stand him, and the feeling seems to be mutual!'

An edited version of this conversation, and her little plot to help save Claddagh, Noelle retailed to her great-aunt, with the strict injuction that not a word of it must ever be revealed to Fergus.

'But it would prove to him how wrong he was about you,' Bridie O'Rourke protested, half laughing, half dismayed by her knowledge.

'I don't have to prove myself to him,' Noelle said proudly. 'If he ever changes his mind, it must be of his own accord. But oh, Aunt, if you could have heard Rachel! She and Manny do so hate parting with money!'

They were both laughing heartily over this comical aspect of Noelle's machinations when Fergus walked in upon them, and at once demanded to share the joke. Their hasty stifling of their mirth, the awkward exchange of glances, and Noelle's mumbled excuse that it was nothing that would amuse him, must have convinced him that their laughter was at his expense.

'I see Miss Browne has completely won you over, Aunt Bridie. I haven't fathomed out her motives yet for being so suddenly co-operative, but believe me, I will.' Brown eyes challenged Noelle to a duel.

'Fergus, Fergus!' his aunt reproached. 'Why are you always so suspicious? Do you never take anyone at face value?'

'Frequently,' he retorted, 'but not Miss Browne, eh, Miss Browne?'

'It seems impossible to please you. Would you rather I demanded my half of our inheritance in cash?'

'Let's say I'd be less surprised!' Fergus drawled.

'Children, children!' Bridie O'Rourke implored, but her plea went unnoticed as the combatants stood almost toe-to-toe, each willing the other to be first to look away.

Noelle was the first to weaken, not because of any lack of conviction in her own integrity, but because the nearness to Fergus was destroying her composure and she could feel a flush, not of guilt but of awareness, suffusing her whole body.

'It would serve you right,' she muttered, 'if I did, and then left you to stew in your own juice, instead of helping.'

Unfairly, Fergus seemed to consider that he had won some moral victory, and as he left the room looking incredibly smug, Noelle felt an uncharacteristic urge to violence, so much so that if anything had been ready to hand, she might have flung it at the back of that departing sable and silver head.

'Oh dear, oh dear!' sighed Miss O'Rourke. 'I do wish you two would get on a little better.' She looked a little pale and distressed and Noelle was immediately contrite.

'I'm sorry, darling, sorry too to cause trouble between you and Fergus. Perhaps it would have been better in the long run if I'd refused to stay?'

'Oh no, please, you must never think that,' Miss O'Rourke assured her hastily. 'I'm sure it will all work out splendidly in the end, and you mustn't worry about me. I can cope with Fergus. Scenes are nothing new in this house. He and my nephew were often at odds.'

Despite Bridie's assurance, Noelle was still a little worried by her pallid looks and a certain shortness of breath in her speech and when she left Bridie O'Rourke, she deliberately went in search of Fergus. She found him, eventually, in the stable-yard and wryly acknowledged to herself that in view of his heredity, she would have saved time by going there first.

The wolfhounds, Cleo and Caesar, were as always at his heels and came to investigate. By now Noelle had schooled herself not to flinch away from them, but she was still tense and nervous in their presence.

'Looking for me?' Fergus said incredulously, the black brows ironically arched. 'I never thought I'd see the day. I thought you couldn't bear the sight of me.'

'I'm not here on my own account, but Aunt Bridie's. Fergus,' belatedly she realised she had broken her vow and used his name, and that he had noticed the fact and her annoyance at her slip, but she went on, 'all this conflict isn't good for her. She was quite upset just now, after we—can't we . . .?' Her voice faltered away as his expression became quizzical.

'Can I believe my ears? You, Noelle, asking for a truce?'

'I told you!' Immediately she was on the defensive. 'It's not for my sake. As far as I'm concerned nothing's changed. But if you have to start an argument, at least do it when Aunt Bridie's not around.' She turned, intending to walk away, but a long arm shot out and she found herself hauled troublingly close to that long, lean body, so that she had to tilt up her head to meet the mocking eyes.

'So we're going to continue fighting, are we? But in private? I think that might be more fun, don't you, Noelle?'

'I don't like quarrels,' she said breathlessly. 'I've always preferred a quiet life.'

'You? A quiet life?' He was shaking that oddly attractive head, the sunlight gleaming on its generous silvering. 'I can't believe that. You're the stormy, tempestuous kind, with that fierce black hair, those sparkling blue eyes. Signs of a passionate nature, Noelle?'

'No,' she denied, 'I'm very even-tempered as a rule. No one has ever made me as furious as——' She stopped in the middle of the dangerous admission as he tilted his own head in interested enquiry.

'As I do?' he finished for her softly.

'It's nothing to be proud of.' She tried wriggling free of his grasp, but the long, lean fingers were very strong. 'You'd irritate a saint.'

'And are you a saint, Noelle Madox-Browne?' His tone was thoughtful. 'So, let's see. You've led a peaceful existence up until now? Just what does that mean, I wonder? No disquiet, no unhappiness perhaps, but maybe no great happiness either. Have you ever been in love, Noelle? Have you ever known passion? Have you ever even been kissed?'

She was finding it harder and harder to control her breathing, to make her limbs stop their ridiculous trembling.

'None of your business,' she managed to say from between clenched teeth.

'Perhaps, perhaps not,' he said obscurely. 'But it would be interesting, academically speaking, to know.'

'You won't find out from me. I——'

'But that's the very source I had in mind!' His words gave absolutely no indication of his intention, and Noelle was caught completely off guard as he swept her into his arms and his mouth came down on hers. 'It's my bet you haven't been kissed like this!'

Contrary to Fergus's expressed belief, Noelle had been kissed before, but not ever with such devastating effect. At the first firm pressure of his lips on hers a flood of sweet fire swept through her, the first shocks of a totally new sensation, and as his clasp upon her deepened into an impassioned embrace she felt a rising tide of response within herself, aware of nothing but his kiss, the strength of his lean body, its hardness locked to hers from mouth to thigh. She felt herself, unbelievably, yielding, and all her senses screamed a protest as firmly he put her away from him, humiliation replacing the frantic desire she had so briefly felt, as she realised she had wanted him to go on, that she had wanted more than just that searing kiss.

'Twenty-five,' he said musingly, 'and yet still virtually unawakened. Where have you been all your life, Noelle? In a convent?'

'No, just in the company of "gentlemen", who don't pounce on women in your wild, rough fashion.' Her tingling lips uttered the words with difficulty, perhaps because of their idiotic tendency to tremble.

'You seemed to be enjoying it,' he said, not a whit abashed.

'Well, I wasn't,' she snapped. In all her life her nerves had never felt so unbearably jangled. 'And if you want my co-operation in restoring Claddagh, don't touch me again!'

'I take it then you've not given further consideration to my proposal?'

'Proposal?' Noelle echoed unwarily, then, her face flushing, 'No, I haven't. I wouldn't waste my time or my energies. I took it how you meant it, as a joke, and one in very poor taste.' She turned away. She didn't want his observant eyes to note the unnatural brightness of hers. Her name on his lips stopped her in her tracks.

'Noelle!' For a wonder his voice was gentle.

'What?' She didn't turn round.

'You're right, about Aunt Bridie, I mean.' He paused, then added, 'I'm glad you feel as you do about her.'

She waited, but nothing more was forthcoming, and a little forlornly she returned to the house.

After this exchange, Noelle felt she must get away for an hour or so, away not from the Hall and its environs, but somewhere, anywhere so she need not encounter Fergus again until these strange symptoms he aroused in her were quelled. Her emotions were totally contradictory. At the same instant as she experienced furious dislike of him, a resentment of the verbal harassments to which he continually subjected her, she felt also the physical pull of his masculinity upon her senses, bemusing her to the point where he was continually in her mind, whether actually present or not. A brisk walk seemed to be the common-sense cure for these vaporous fancies, and she set out determinedly in the direction of the lough.

The day was beautifully mild, though drifting clouds and shafts of changing light alternately touched the soft hazy colours of the countryside. As Noelle had already noticed from her bedroom window which overlooked the lough, its aspect too was constantly changing, at one moment its surface a burnished jewel reflecting the mottled sky, the next a patina of textured ripples.

She turned for an instant to look back at the house with its backdrop of mountains, all around it fields, great swards of grassland in a multitude of greens sprinkled with the confetti of buttercups, walled by stone boundaries that kept in the sleek, well groomed animals that grazed there.

Not far from the lough side, and still, surely, on Claddagh property, stood a small thatched cottage. In spite of the mild day, a thin line of blue smoke rose from its chimney. Miss O'Rourke had told Noelle that these cottages still abounded in Ireland, not as a tourist gimmick, but because both people of the older generation and some of the young people preferred to live in them.

Curiosity took Noelle's steps in that direction, and as she drew closer, she saw the figure of a man leaning in the doorway watching her.

'Good morning to you!' The man's voice was pleasant, with only the slightest hint of a brogue, but his eyes and whole stance were wary. 'You'll be the new young lady from the Hall, I'm thinking?'

'Yes, I was admiring your cottage. I hope I'm not trespassing?'

He gave a short laugh.

'Sure, and doesn't the very soil this place stands on belong to yourself and Mr Fergus Carrick?'

'You're a tenant?'

'You could put it like that.' His reply seemed deliberately evasive.

'It's a lovely place,' Noelle ventured placatingly.

'Want to see inside?'

'Please, if it's no trouble.'

He jerked his head for her to precede him.

Inside, the cottage was much as she had been led to expect, a two-room, single-storey structure, with a peat fire burning on an open hearth, the chimney in the centre of the building, even though, as Noelle's keen eyes soon detected, mains electricity was laid on. Nor was it lacking in other home comforts, being well if somewhat sparsely furnished, a bachelor's dwelling if Noelle was any judge, functional and lacking unnecessary ornamentation.

'Patrick Byrne,' he introduced himself, holding out a broad freckled hand.

'Noelle Madox-Browne,' she returned.

'You'll take some refreshment?' he enquired. 'Tea? Coffee?'

'Oh no, really. I don't want to impose. I just——'

'But of course, you wouldn't want to be socialising with one of the tenants.' His voice had taken on a bitter note. 'This will be just in the nature of an inspection of your property. And what have they been telling you about me, I wonder, the folks up at the big house?'

Noelle summed up the situation immediately. This was a proud man, in some way dependent on the residents of Claddagh Hall and clearly resenting it. Uninvited she sat down.

'I didn't even know of your existence, Mr Byrne, or that there was a cottage here. I merely intended to walk as far as the lough, and I'll gladly accept your hospitality, if I'm not intruding on your time?'

He weighed her up narrowly for a moment, then his fresh features relaxed and he ran one of his broad hands through tow-coloured hair, an almost boyish gesture, accompanied as it was by a self-deprecating laugh.

'Forgive me now if I seem a little sensitive on the subject, but 'tis only fair to tell you that those at the Hall, particularly Fergus Carrick, wouldn't approve of you being here, associating with me.'

'I make my own friends,' Noelle said firmly, 'without any reference to Fergus.'

'Oh?' His sandy brows lifted quizzically. 'Yet there's talk about that you two are to be married, to keep the property intact.'

'Mr Byrne, I have no idea who's been spreading such rumours, but I can tell you they're totally unfounded. It's true Mr Carrick and I inherited the property jointly, but there our association ends.'

'I see.' A smile banished the remaining doubt

from his face. 'In that case perhaps *we* can be friends?'

'I don't see why not, and now,' briskly, 'didn't you mention something about a cup of tea?'

'Indeed I did, unless—have you ever tried Irish coffee?'

'Once, some time ago.'

'But never in Ireland, made by a true Irishman, with real Irish whiskey?' and at her laughing assent, 'Will you try it now?'

Having agreed, Noelle asked to be allowed to watch him prepare it. This also gave her an opportunity to study her host more closely, but unobserved. He was just how she had always imagined a typical Irishman would be, stocky of stature, rugged of countenance. He made black coffee, to which he added plenty of brown sugar, a fact that made Noelle wince, for she hadn't a sweet tooth, and a measure of whiskey. Then he poured cream over the back of a spoon, so that it floated on the top.

'Drink it through the cream,' he advised, as he handed her the cup. 'Well?' after a few moments in which Noelle found herself unexpectedly enjoying the drink despite its sweetness.

'A unique experience,' she told him, and he smiled with satisfaction.

'I told you it takes an Irishman to make a good cup of Irish coffee.'

Fearing to outstay her welcome, Noelle set down her cup and rose to leave, and Patrick Byrne seemed disappointed.

'But you'll come again and we'll have a good crack?'

'Thank you, I'd like that,' she said truthfully. It had been restful to be in the company of a man who did not disturb her composure, against whom she need not be continually on her guard.

'All the same,' he said in parting, 'I wouldn't say anything up at the Hall, about our meeting.'

But Noelle wasn't in the habit of lying or of concealment, and when Miss O'Rourke enquired mildly, in Fergus's presence, whether she enjoyed her walk and where it had taken her, she replied frankly.

'Down by the lough. I discovered a very picturesque cottage and met the man who lives there.'

'Patrick Byrne?' Fergus rapped out the question.

'Yes.' Steadily Noelle met brown eyes suddenly angry. 'I take it you know him?'

'Oh, I know Patrick Byrne all right. A pity you didn't tell me where you were going. I'd have warned you to keep away from him.'

'If you had I wouldn't have taken any notice,' she retorted, 'and Patrick told me you'd——'

'Oh, so it's Patrick, is it, already, when you can't even bring yourself to use *my* name, except by accident.'

'I only call my friends by their first names.'

'And you think Byrne wants to be a friend to you? You're crazy! He'll have his eye on the main chance, your share of Claddagh.'

'You're the one who's crazy,' snapped Noelle, 'I

only met the man for the first time today.'

'Only because you called on him. He knows he'd better not set foot across this threshold.'

'Then I'll invite him here and there's nothing you can do about it.'

'You think not? How about if I throw him out, neck and crop?'

What a ridiculous argument they had got into, forgetting all their resolutions, Noelle reflected some moments later, after Fergus had stamped out with the bitter remark that he would sooner endure marriage himself, even to such a virago, than see O'Rourke property fall into Patrick Byrne's hands. Until Fergus had begun laying down the law, the idea of inviting Patrick to return her visit hadn't even occurred to her. She wasn't that much interested in the man, but his acquaintance could be a useful stick to beat Fergus with. She put the tempting thought aside for the moment and apologised to Miss O'Rourke.

'Sorry, Aunt Bridie. I had meant to avoid rows with Fergus in front of you. I know it upsets you.'

Her great-aunt smiled faintly.

'I'm not quite such a delicate plant, my dear, and all the O'Rourkes tend to be hot-blooded. It seems you and Fergus are no exception.'

Manny Cohen's awaited visit, which was to help restore Claddagh's fallen fortunes, only prompted another clash between the cousins. First Noelle had to set the scene, and this she did by producing, one evening, the three paintings she had unearthed from one of the attics.

'I'm not certain, of course,' she said, carefully casual, 'but I think they might be rather good ones. I've seen something very similar in a collection owned by a friend of mine. I've asked him to come over and take a look at them.'

'By what right?' Fergus demanded. 'Why didn't you consult me first?'

'What use would that have been? You admitted you knew nothing about art, and I have a friend who does. You *were* hoping to sell something to pay the bills?' she challenged, and Fergus couldn't deny it.

Since he already knew he would be taking the pictures back to London with him, Manny Cohen had brought his car over and, as Noelle had done, driven cross-country to Galway. Notified of his expected time of arrival, Noelle was on the lookout for him, and as the tall, slightly stooped figure emerged from his car, she flew out to intercept him, to remind him of his script and that he should be careful what he said in front of Fergus.

'What name am I to give?' Manny enquired anxiously, and laughingly Noelle told him his own.

'The less acting you have to do the better,' she advised. 'Just be yourself, but rave about the pictures!'

Manny looked doubtful, but promised to do his best, and he succeeded so well that Fergus became suspicious. He took Noelle on one side.

'If he's so damned keen to buy those pictures at that price, they must be worth a hell of a lot more. How do we know he's not taking us for a ride?'

'Because I trust him,' Noelle snapped. Surely

Fergus wasn't going to play hard to get and ruin all her plans. If he insisted on a second opinion and a real expert came down from London, her well-meaning deceit would be exposed.

'Know him well, do you?' Fergus enquired.

'As it happens, yes!' She met his gaze steadily and after a while he jerked his head in agreement.

'All right. I admit I know nothing about paintings. He's the expert and I won't deny the money will be useful, an unexpected bonus of your acquaintance,' he concluded satirically.

Noelle bit back a retort. This wasn't the moment to renew hostilities. Even now it wasn't too late for him to have second thoughts about the sale of the pictures.

The deal concluded and the pictures carefully installed in the boot of Manny's car, Noelle went outside to see him off.

'Did I do it right?' he enquired anxiously.

'Hush!' with a nervous glance over her shoulder. 'Yes, you did fine. Sure you won't stay overnight?'

'Quite sure. That cousin of yours makes me nervous. I was waiting for him to ask me something I couldn't answer. No, I'll put up somewhere along the way.'

'Well, thanks, Manny. I really appreciate your help.' She stood on tiptoe to kiss his cheek. 'Give my love to Rachel. Tell her I'll be over to see her as soon as I can.'

'So you do know him pretty well,' said Fergus, having witnessed this scene from the window.

'I said I did,' she replied composedly.

'Just how well, I wonder?' he said as if to himself.

'He must be well off, able to fork out such an astronomical sum for three tatty-looking old pictures.' It had been decided after all that Manny should be a private buyer rather than from any well-known firm.

'I don't know him in the way you're trying to imply,' Noelle was provoked into saying. 'For one thing, he's a married man.'

'So was Lissadell,' Fergus retorted, 'but that didn't make any difference, or *you* wouldn't be here now.'

Noelle lost her temper and all caution. She advanced upon him.

'Will you stop throwing that at me every time we have a disagreement!' and as his face still wore its mocking expression, she aimed a blow at him.

To her surprise, it made contact, and she felt against her palm the not disagreeable sensation of coarse facial hair. Moreover a swift movement of his own hand had trapped hers there, so that she was compelled to go on enduring the sensation.

Unbeknown to herself, her eyes had widened in wonder, and Fergus gazed steadily into their depths as he moved his head slightly, so that now it was his mouth that brushed her sensitive palm, making a shudder race through her.

'Would you rather we kissed and made friends?' he murmured against her hand, so that his warm breath was itself a caress.

Noelle tried to retrieve her hand, and, finding it impossible, tried to answer him with cool dignity.

'I should certainly prefer it if we could behave in a civilised manner towards each other. Goodness knows I've tried, but you must be the most irritating, deliberately offensive man I've ever met!'

'Is that so?' he enqured interestedly. 'And I thought you were entirely indifferent to me.'

'I am—I mean, apart from the fact that you annoy me.'

'Of course.' His expression was devastatingly dead-pan. 'What else would I be implying?' To her relief, he released her, but she was totally unprepared for the subsequent feeling of loss she experienced when her hand was freed from his clasp.

'Since we're selling off the dross to improve the quality of the whole,' Fergus said a few days later, 'I'm thinking of getting rid of some of the horses. There won't be room for them all, in any case, when I bring my own stock over.'

'You've definitely decided to sell up in England, then? Won't your family have something to say about that, your friends?'

'My parents are no longer alive, and if you're asking in an oblique way if there's a woman in my life ...?' Seen in profile, his beard made it difficult to tell whether or not his mouth had curved in its usual mockery.

'I wasn't,' she denied, 'nothing of the sort.'

'Well, I'll tell you anyway, just in case. There isn't, at least no one special woman. If there were, do you think I'd have proposed to you?'

Noelle stopped in her tracks, facing him squarely, hands on hips.

'Let's get this straight, once and for all, shall we?

I'm not interested in your private life. I couldn't care less whether you have half a dozen women, let alone one, and you didn't propose to me. I don't call that a proper proposal and I refuse to treat such a stupidly insulting joke seriously.' She turned on her heel and marched on towards the stableyard. 'Which horses are you thinking of selling?'

To her relief, he followed her lead.

'The hunters for a start. I don't hunt, do you?' and as she shook her head, 'You'll notice I do you the courtesy of consulting you first, not like you with the oil paintings and your rich boyfriend.'

Noelle decided to ignore this taunt. She was beginning to discover that Fergus positively enjoyed annoying her. Well, she was going to deprive him of that satisfaction.

'Which others do you suggest?'

Fergus was just about to answer, when a large horsebox rattled into the yard, pulling up a few feet from where they stood. The driver jumped down, consulting a piece of paper.

'Mr Carrick, is it? Two bay hunters to be collected for Mr O'Shea of Ballinashloe!'

'So you consulted me first, did you,' Noelle muttered *sotto voce*, further infuriated by the guileless, insouciant grin that met her accusing stare. He hadn't an ounce of shame about him, she thought angrily. Of all the hypocritical . . .

'You're a day early,' Fergus told the driver as they moved towards the loose-boxes. The man looked surprised.

'Sure, and isn't it Thursday, then?' and as Fergus shook his head, 'Well, all the saints be blessed! Am

I not after doing it again!' Then his tone altered. 'Watch out for yourself there then, miss.' His warning came too late.

Lost in her thoughts, Noelle hadn't noticed Caesar pad into the yard, and as a cold, wet nose explored her hand, she had let out a shriek of alarm. As she did so, one of the hunters threw up his head, pulling the halter from the driver's hand. Finding itself temporarily unrestrained, the horse bolted, barging her aside, knocking her to the cobbled surface of the yard.

'Noelle! For God's sake!' Fergus bent over her, his face white beneath its tan. 'Are you hurt?'

'I—I don't think so.' Shakily she began to rise, and as the fear faded from Fergus's face, anger replaced it.

'Don't you know better than to scream when you're standing right under the hoofs of a spirited horse?'

'It wasn't my fault,' Noelle retorted, 'it was that great grey monster of yours!' Her defiance wavered as Fergus's face seemed to swim distortedly before her eyes. Then everything went black.

CHAPTER FOUR

WHAT on earth was Fergus doing in her bedroom, sitting on the edge of her bed? Then Noelle remembered, she had fainted. He must have carried her up here.

'Any pain anywhere?' he asked, as her eyes focused and met his.

'It was just my ankle. I think I must have twisted it when I fell.'

'Let me see.'

'No, really, I'll be all right. I'll put a cold compress on it and . . .'

But he was totally ignoring her protests, long, sensitive fingers probing, examining.

'That hurt, or that?'

'It's a little tender, but honestly, I don't think it's anything serious.'

'Good.' But he did not remove his hand. Instead, as if absently, his fingers now lightly caressed, seemed as if they would begin to move upward.

Noelle tensed immediately and sat up. It was unbearable to know this lovely urgency caused by his hands and to know that she must deter him from any further intimacy. But her movements had brought her face close to his, too close.

'I'd like to get up,' she said unsteadily.

'What's the hurry?' he murmured. 'You need to rest. You might still be suffering from shock, or you might have other injuries we haven't discovered yet.' He abandoned his exploration of her ankle and took her hands, turning them this way and that. 'No grazes or bruises there.'

'I told you,' Noelle's nerves were at screaming point, 'I'm O.K.'

He seemed to be peculiarly afflicted by deafness, for he took no notice of her protestations, his hands sliding up her arms to her shoulders, slipping into niches between shoulder and throat that proved shockingly sensitive to his touch.

She couldn't seem to keep her eyes from his, as he bent his head, coming nearer.

'Noelle, my dear, I believe there's been some kind of accident? Siobhan said——' Miss O'Rourke hurried in, one hand held to her breast in breathless agitation. At the scene before her, she stopped, confused.

Noelle, aware of her own flushed face and tremulous limbs, evaded Fergus's grasp and went to her great-aunt.

'You shouldn't have hurried up all those stairs!' she scolded. 'Sit down for a moment. I'm perfectly all right.'

Fergus seemed totally unabashed by the situation in which they had been discovered, taking his time in rising from the bed, strolling towards the door.

'I can vouch for that, Aunt Bridie. Noelle's all right!'

They both glanced at him sharply. There had been some sort of subtle nuance in his voice that neither understood, but his expression gave nothing away.

'If you'll both excuse me, I'll get back to the yard. Can't trust those young stable lads to work without supervision.'

'Which means,' Bridie O'Rourke said fondly, as the door closed behind him, 'that he'll be working alongside them, as hard and perhaps harder than they do.' Then, with a sly upward glance at Noelle, 'I'm sorry I interrupted just now, but I was anxious——'

'You weren't interrupting anything at all,' Noelle said hastily. 'Fergus was just making sure I wasn't hurt.'

'Oh?' The word held a wealth of meaning. 'Just as you say, dear, but I could've sworn he was just about to kiss you.'

'No! I mean, well, I wouldn't have let him. I was very glad you came in.' Liar, Noelle thought dismally. The last thing in her mind had been the hope of interruption, all her concentration had been upon those gipsyish features coming closer, the relaxed warmth of his mouth so near to hers. She changed the subject. 'I'd better get back to my own work. I'm sorting through the attics, trying to decide what stuff's worth keeping and what needs throwing out. It's in an appalling muddle.'

'My dear.' Bridie O'Rourke paused as they parted on the landing. 'Would it be such a bad thing if Fergus were to fall in love with you?'

For a stunned moment, Noelle stared at her, eyes wide. It wouldn't be such a bad thing at all, she discovered, but it wasn't likely to happen. The near-embrace Miss O'Rourke had witnessed hadn't been an expression of tenderness on Fergus's part, any more than his repeated suggestions of marriage had been indications of love. If Fergus did want to marry her, and she doubted the strength of that inclination, it was only for one reason, to make sure that Claddagh remained intact and in his grasp. For if she were to marry anyone else, it would make life difficult for Fergus, since he would never have full control over the estate. Noelle was quite certain that if he had been in a position to buy her out, there would have been no talk of marriage.

She had been so lost in thought she hadn't answered her great-aunt's question, and yet Bridie was nodding as if somehow satisfied before turning away towards her own room.

Rummaging about amongst the hoarded miscellany of other people's lives was a fascinating, albeit grubby task. Noelle worked systematically, dividing her finds into those things to be retained or examined further and those to be discarded.

Fergus came upon her there, so engrossed that she did not hear his approach, and he leant against a rafter, studying her absorbed face.

It was a nice little face, he mused, if unspectacular. At least it was nice to outward appearance, but who knew what deviousness lay beneath the surface? The features, pointed chin, small, decidedly tip-tilted nose, were puckish and at times infuriatingly provocative. When she smiled, which was rarely in his presence, her mouth made a mischievous triangle, making her otherwise unremarkable face oddly attractive. For convenience, she had tied back her long dark hair in a jaunty pony-tail, making her look far younger than her twenty-five years. The jeans and T-shirt she wore emphasised her whipcord slenderness, the soft swell of small but perfectly shaped breasts, and Fergus felt a stirring within him.

He wished he knew just why she had changed her mind and decided to stay, when to refuse would certainly have meant the sale of Claddagh and its value in her pocket. But she remained provokingly reticent on the subject.

'Did you know you have cobwebs in your hair?' he asked, startling her.

'No, but I'm not surprised.' She strove to recover her equanimity. Drat the man. Couldn't he leave her in peace for a moment, especially while she came to terms with this new knowledge pulsating within her, that what she had considered to be a purely physical response to his masculinity, his unconventional good looks, had become something deeper, that she was dangerously near to falling in love with Fergus Carrick. 'I should think we're the first people for years to disturb this lot,' she went on, determined to maintain her cool, remote manner, which she decided must be her future attitude if she was not to betray herself to him.

'Let me brush them away. They make you look prematurely grey.'

He didn't wait for permission, his long fingers delicately performing their self-appointed task. Though his touch on her hair was feather-light, Noelle was shudderingly aware of it, of his physical nearness, an electric sensation that seemed to her to raise all the fine downy hairs on her arms, the nape of her neck, so that she was sure the effect must be visible to the man who produced it.

Cobwebs removed, Fergus dipped his head and brushed his lips across her nape.

'You should wear your hair up more often,' he said huskily. 'Pity to hide such a beautiful neck and throat.' As he spoke of her throat, one hand came up to clasp about it, and Noelle's skin, already hypersensitive with excitement, burnt and tingled.

What had begun as a helpful gesture had become something more—or had he intended all along that this should happen? This was no mere caress now. She knew the difference between that and what he had begun to do with his strong fingers. He had found the unmistakable arousal of her breasts and his hands stayed to tantalise still further, before travelling on in a maddening, delirium-making route over and down to her hips.

Without being aware that either of them had moved, she found herself caught against the hard curve of his body, his mouth on hers, the heat of his kiss penetrating beyond her lips, searing downwards, affecting the rest of her body. Inside, desire burnt and tortured, so that she clung to him in an eruption of hunger she could not hide, feeling the thrust of his own urge.

It was only as he manoeuvred her towards an old chaise-longue, relegated to the attic by some past O'Rourke, that sanity returned, and, gasping for air, she pushed him away.

'No, Fergus, no. Let me go!'

Somewhat to her surprise, he released her immediately, but in the light cast by the one naked lamp, she could see that his eyes still smouldered.

'Why have you come up here?' She backed away from him, her hands going automatically to tidy hair and clothing.

'We were interrupted before.' His voice was unsteadier than hers, she noted with satisfaction.

'For which I was thankful. So you thought you'd corner me up here, where nobody else ever goes?'

'Something like that,' he agreed, but his voice was controlled now, with its usual light mockery in evidence. 'I find myself wanting to test this claim of yours that you're totally immune to me, and I must tell you, I don't believe it.'

'That,' she snapped, 'is because you're thoroughly conceited. You've probably been used to women who run to you the moment you crook your finger. I've got more pride, more self-control.'

'So,' he watched her narrowly, 'you admit it *takes* self-control to ward me off?'

'I admit nothing. You're just very good at taking people by surprise. You're also stronger than I am. But that doesn't mean——'

'No, it doesn't, does it,' he sounded suddenly bored by the subject, 'and in fact I really came up here to tell you to clean yourself up and change. We're going out.'

'Just like that?' Noelle exploded. 'You expect me to just drop what I'm doing and——'

'In the interests of Claddagh, yes. Because that *is* all you're interested in, isn't it, Noelle? I've a theory about you.' It was a new gambit which had just occurred to him. 'I think I know now why you're being so unexpectedly co-operative, despite your obvious dislike of me. If we can manage to put Claddagh back on its feet, make a going concern of it, it will eventually fetch more at sale, won't it?' From under half closed lids he watched her reaction.

Noelle was hurt, particularly in view of all she knew she had already done for the Hall, but if he wanted to think that way, let him. At least it might prevent any repetition of his calculated, insincere lovemaking, which would have been easier to endure if she had been totally indifferent to him.

'I'd be taking a bit of a gamble, wouldn't I?'

'Not really. To the have-nots, a few thousand pounds is better than nothing.'

Yes, he still thought she was a penniless mercenary. Noelle was fiercely glad she had never revealed her background to him. But one day, one glorious day of reckoning, she was going to do just that, and take great pleasure in seeing him grovel. That Fergus Carrick was not exactly the type to grovel didn't enter into her considerations.

'My offer's still open,' she told him, 'for you to buy me out, now.'

'And you know damned well I can't afford to do that.' Then, 'Come on, or we'll be late.'

'I haven't said I'm coming yet. Why should I?'

He grabbed her arm and propelled her through the loft space and down to the bedroom floor.

'Last time I made a sale, to help our finances, you made a crack about not being consulted, even though you'd just done something similar. So this time, you're being advised in advance. We're going to see our neighbours. They're willing to buy up some of Claddagh's stock and you're going to be there, so you can't accuse me of cheating you of your share in the deal. Fair enough?'

The Faheys, the O'Rourkes' nearest neighbours, were rich. That much was evident to Noelle even as Fergus's car approached the large boundary wall with a lodge at either end. Once inside the great iron gates, a drive curved around through ancient trees concealing until the last moment a long, low mansion with a pillared portico. To one side there were stables with a little belfry as well as barns and various other farm buildings.

Mr Fahey was a slim, horsey-faced man of middle age, clothed in riding breeches and a rough tweed jacket. He was not, according to Fergus, a racing man, but ran a pony trekking establishment and riding school. He was interested in buying up the less promising colts and fillies from the Claddagh Stud.

In the library, business was concluded over drinks, Mr Fahey pouring out two enormous whiskies, to which he added the merest teaspoonful of water. Noelle had refused a drink and Fergus, she noticed, barely touched his, except in polite response to his host's 'good health'. The transaction over, nothing would suit Mr Fahey but that they meet the rest of his family, and accordingly he led them through the house to the enclosed rear garden.

Noelle cast slightly envious eyes over the impeccable decorative order of the house, its well-cared-for antique furnishings. But Claddagh would be like this again some day, she vowed.

Mrs Fahey, or Maeve, as she insisted they call
her, was a buxom, pleasant, rosy-cheeked woman,
but it was her daughter, Suzanne, who caught the
awed interest of both visitors.

Suzanne Fahey, Noelle decided, must be around
her own age, maybe even a little older, but it just
wasn't fair, she thought, all too aware of Fergus's
instinctive male reactions, that one person should
be endowed with so many attributes.

Tall and statuesque, generously proportioned,
she made Noelle feel dwarf-like. She had fair hair
that gleamed and curled, satin skin delicately
tinted, large, winsome violet eyes and an irresistible
smile that widened to reveal pearl-white teeth.

'And a friend of Suzanne's, Mr Byrne,' Maeve
Fahey introduced.

'Patrick, how nice!'

'Noelle and I have already met.'

They both spoke at once and as Noelle held out
her hand to Patrick Byrne, she was conscious of
Fergus's taut disapproval and that the Faheys were
puzzled when each man barely acknowledged the
other's presence.

Cordially, Maeve invited Noelle and Fergus to
stay for high tea, but to Noelle's surprise, Fergus
refused. Judging by his reaction to Suzanne, the
close conversation in which he had engaged her,
Noelle would have expected him to jump at the
chance of furthering the acquaintance. It must have
been due to Patrick's presence, she decided. For as
the Faheys saw them to their car, Fergus accepted
an invitation for Noelle and himself to dine in the
near future.

'Did you have to be so rude to Patrick?' Noelle demanded as they drove away. 'What's he ever done to you? Or more to the point, what have you done to him?'

'I don't follow. What makes you think I've harmed the fellow?'

'Because, as a general rule, people are most violent in their dislike of someone they've injured.'

'Quite the little philosopher, aren't you? I suppose this championship of Byrne wouldn't be because you happen to have taken a fancy to him, whereas you haven't a good word for me?'

'Yes, as it happens, I do like Patrick. He's quiet and polite, whereas you . . .'

'All right, I get the message. But don't be fooled by Byrne's milk-and-water manner. He resents the pair of us, but you being a woman, he obviously believes it more to his advantage to keep on good terms.'

'Why should he resent us?' Noelle recalled Patrick's prickly manner at their first encounter, which she had put down to a proud man's fear of patronage from the 'big house'.

'Because, my dear Noelle, but for a small formality, it would be him living at Claddagh instead of in one of the estate cottages.' He angled a glance at her, and seeing her total incomprehension: 'Byrne was his mother's name. Maureen Byrne was the daughter of the head lad at Claddagh. That was when my mother was a girl. Maureen ran away with the black sheep of the O'Rourke family, Seamus, Noel's young brother. Patrick is the outcome of that association, but, as

Seamus neglected to marry his mother——'

'You mean, if he had, Patrick would have been the legal heir to Claddagh. He would have been Lord Lissadell? Oh, how unfair!'

Fergus braked sharply, leaving the engine idling as he turned fully to look at her.

'Now don't go feeling sorry for him. Why do women always seem to think with their emotions? Pity's no foundation for a relationship anyway.'

'But it isn't fair,' Noelle maintained. 'If we're talking about legitimacy, and that's what it amounts to, Patrick has as much right at Claddagh as I have.'

'Except that you're the daughter of the elder son.'

'I still think that some provision should have been made for him,' she said stubbornly.

'Women! Give me strength!' muttered Fergus. 'Look, don't get the wrong idea about Byrne. He doesn't have to live in that picturesque hovel on O'Rourke land. My uncle Seamus made a fortune in mining, and when he died he left everything to his natural son. Byrne is rolling in it. That's one of the reasons I'd hate to see Claddagh up for sale. He'd buy it like a shot.'

'Then why does he live in the cottage?'

'To be a thorn in the side of the O'Rourkes, why else? That cottage was his mother's home originally. When Byrne came back to England a few years ago, he made himself known to my uncle and, as Lissadell had no children, practically demanded to be made his heir.'

'There was no doubt he's who he says he is, I suppose?'

'None at all, unfortunately. Anyway, Lissadell refused point blank to acknowledge him. There was no love lost between him and his brother Seamus. Some people even said Noel fancied Maureen Byrne himself. He certainly said he'd no intention of seeing any bastard of Seamus's living at Claddagh. The only concession he was prepared to make was that Byrne should have the cottage, and I doubt he'd have agreed to that if he'd known how well heeled the fellow was. He found out too late, by which time Byrne had got himself dug in.'

Fergus re-engaged the gears and they moved on, Noelle quietly thoughtful. Neither of them spoke again until she alighted from the car in the stableyard.

'Just remember, Noelle, Byrne would do anything to get a foot across the threshold of Claddagh. He'd even go so far as to marry you.'

'And that would be a terrible hardship for any man!' she retorted angrily.

'Did I say that?'

'You didn't have to. You've been implying it ever since we met. And,' she turned back towards him, 'what makes you any better than Patrick? You've openly admitted that even you would stoop to marry me, to gain full control here.'

Fergus rounded the car. He was angry, one dismayed glance told her that. Nervously she looked around. Evening stables were over, the lads gone home to their tea. There was no one in sight.

'I don't recall the word "stoop" ever being used, but yes, I did suggest we got married. It seemed a sensible solution in more ways than one. Aunt

Bridie can't live for ever, and when she goes, we'll be here alone, unchaperoned.'

'When that happens, and I hope it won't be for a very long time—I happen to love Aunt Bridie—I'll probably have had enough of your company anyway, and I may have decided to marry someone else. Certainly I shall never marry unless I'm in love with the man.'

'Marry someone else? Who? Byrne? Because if it is ...'

'Fergus, for goodness' sake! I've met Patrick Byrne twice. Hardly grounds for a romantic attachment to have formed. But if it ever does, that will be my affair and his.'

'You couldn't marry that cold-blooded, calculating fish, because that's what he is. There's no fire, no warmth in the man, not even in an argument. A man like that isn't for you. He'd suffocate you. And I'll see him at the bottom of Galway Bay before he enters this house as your husband.'

If only she could believe Fergus's fervent statement to be one of jealousy, instead of determination that the other man should have no claim upon Claddagh, as he certainly would if he married Noelle! It would serve Fergus right in a way, for all his taunting of her, if she did encourage Patrick, if she did fall in love with the other man. But then only Noelle knew that was utterly impossible, at least at the moment, given the way Fergus himself affected her.

'But I'm supposed to stand by, without a word of criticism or complaint, when you come home some day with a wife? And I don't have to look very far to guess who it will be, do I?'

Fergus chuckled.

'You mean Suzanne? Jealous, Noelle?'

She was, but she wasn't admitting it.

'Certainly not. I'm just pointing out that I've as much right to cultivate Patrick as you have to cultivate Suzanne. The moment you met you were . . . what's wrong?' For Fergus was openly laughing at her.

'That wasn't our first meeting though I admit we've not met for some time. She's an old friend. I've known Sue since I first came here. She was a skinny, leggy schoolgirl then.' He chuckled. 'She's certainly changed over the years.'

'Oh!' Noelle felt deflated and a little foolish, but she remained adamant in her rejection of Fergus's right to monitor her private life, and she deliberately sought out Patrick Byrne again a few days later. She tried to tell herself that she was only curious, wanting to learn more about him from his own lips. After all, they had a common bond in their parentage.

Patrick was surprised to see her and said so bluntly.

'Good morning. I thought you'd have been warned off me by the new Lord of the Manor.'

'I was, but I'm not taking any notice of that, and he isn't Lord of the Manor. As far as that goes, we have equal rights, and I want you to know I think it's a shame my father didn't make any acknowledgement of you in his will.'

'Do you, indeed?' There was a calculating look in his eye which might have disturbed Noelle had she noticed it. 'Of course,' he went on, 'I would have been in a better position than Fergus Carrick to restore Claddagh. What is he, after all, but a small-time farmer?'

'He knows about horses, too.' In spite of everything, Noelle felt compelled to defend Fergus.

'Of course, of course,' he said placatingly, 'but there's not enough money to be made from horses to run a place of that size. What you both need,' he went on with a casual laugh that deceived Noelle into thinking he was joking, 'since you say you've no thought of marriage to each other, is to find rich partners, willing to plough their money into the estate. Now if, say, you were to marry me, or Fergus were to marry Suzanne——'

'But that's not likely, of course!' Noelle said sharply, at the vivid recollection of the other girl's beauty. Although Fergus had known Suzanne for ages, he hadn't denied that he might be considering her as a possible wife.

'Maybe, maybe not,' said Patrick, 'it was just a "for instance".'

But his words had set Noelle thinking again, and suddenly it seemed imperative that she get back to the Hall. Where was Fergus now? His company, she realised, however abrasive, was infinitely preferable to his absence, especially if that absence took him to the Faheys. She made the excuse that it was nearly lunchtime,

'Even so, you'd better stay a while longer, I'm thinking,' Patrick advised. 'It's blowing up for a squall. Look at the lough.'

Noelle did so, and saw the wild grey curtains of

rain sweeping across its surface, hiding from view the tree-girt islands. Soon a thick and thunderous downpour was setting the clouds rumbling overhead.

'And it was so nice a moment ago,' she marvelled.

'Sure, it's fickle weather we have here,' Patrick agreed, 'but I'll not be complaining about it today, since it means you'll have to stay a while longer.'

Noelle eyed him uneasily. She had cultivated Patrick, not with the intention of annoying Fergus, but out of her sense of fair play, but she hoped her friendly manner—for that was all it was—wouldn't give Patrick the wrong idea. At her contriving they talked inconsequentialities, but for all that she was relieved when, from the window, she saw a mighty rainbow arch itself across the lough, which now glistened in the thin, bright light that followed the rain.

However, she was not to escape so easily— Patrick announcing his intention of accompanying her.

'Really there's no need,' she protested.

'Does there have to be a need?' he asked reproachfully. 'I feel like a breath of fresh air and the pleasure of your company.'

'What do you find to do all day?' Noelle asked him as they strolled over the rain-fresh grass.

'Do? You mean work, I suppose? Have *they* been telling you what an idle fellow I am? And why not? Life passes by quickly enough without filling every moment. I fish a little—there's fine salmon to be had in the lough. I walk, and when I'm in the mood I write.'

'You're a writer? What sort of things do you write?'

Patrick gave a grunt of laughter.

'I've no claim to be an author, since I've had nothing published. But I'm working on a history of the O'Rourkes, tracing the family tree. On which,' he added bitterly, 'my name will appear with a bar sinister.'

'That really worries you, doesn't it?' Noelle said wonderingly. 'Yet I'm in the same position and I find it doesn't matter. We're not to blame for what our parents did.'

'My dear girl, 'tis not the morals of the case that concern me. What really irks me is to see Fergus Carrick lording it on property which, but for a slight technicality, should have been mine.'

'And do you resent me too, Patrick?' she asked quietly.

He regarded her thoughtfully, then reached out a square, freckled hand and took one of hers.

'D'you know, I don't. But somehow it's different. Maybe because you're a woman, and a very attractive one, and maybe because of your birth. It pleases me to see Carrick having to divide everything with you. How does he like that, by the way?'

'He doesn't.'

They walked on, and somehow Patrick seemed not to realise that he still held her hand.

'You asked me how I occupy myself, what about you? You must have had a job of some kind, in England? Did you give it up?'

'No.' Noelle deliberated whether she should tell

him the truth about herself, then decided against it. The fewer people who knew the better. Patrick was friendly with the Faheys and what they knew might get back to Fergus. 'But I had some holiday owing to me, six weeks, so I took it all at once.'

'Then you'll be going back eventually?'

'I don't know. That's something I have to decide.' Noelle had pretty well made up her mind what she was going to do, but again she didn't intend to confide in Patrick Byrne.

By now they were within sight of the Hall, and he stopped.

'I suppose I'd best be leaving you now? You'll not be wanting Carrick to see us together?'

'But only because our endless rows upset Aunt Bridie,' Noelle told him. 'She's old and rather frail.'

'I'll be seeing you again, will I? Maybe we could go out some evening?' He squeezed her hand, and, leaning forward, kissed her cheek. 'Till next time, Noelle,' and at her startled, querying glance, 'after all, we are cousins!'

His discretion, however, was wasted. As Noelle breasted the last undulating swell of turf, she saw Fergus standing, arms folded, legs widely planted, glaring down over the lough. There was no chance that he hadn't witnessed that affectionate farewell, and Noelle braced herself for conflict, so it was with almost a sense of deflation that she realised Fergus wasn't going to say anything about seeing her and Patrick together.

'Lunch is on the table,' he said curtly, 'and Aunt Bridie waiting!'

As if to point up the needlessness of Fergus's

reproof, Miss O'Rourke, already placidly eating, showed surprise at Noelle's apology.

'Don't worry, dear. I'm quite accustomed to people coming in at odd hours for their food. Sometimes poor Noel forgot altogether.'

Noelle looked pointedly at Fergus, and he met her accusing stare with an enigmatic steadiness which led her to suspect that he hadn't been searching for her because a meal was ready, but because he had suspected her of visiting the cottage by the lough and had been waiting to have his suspicions confirmed. Well, she hoped he was satisfied. How dared he spy on her? But Miss O'Rourke was still speaking and Noelle forced herself to pay attention.

'All the same, I'm glad Fergus found you. It would have been a shame if you'd missed what he has in store for you.'

CHAPTER FIVE

NOELLE couldn't restrain an apprehensive glance in Fergus's direction. What was he up to now? She couldn't think of any plans he might have that boded her any good.

'I have to go into Galway this afternoon. I've an appointment at the bank. I thought you might like to come along for the ride, do a little shopping? To my certain knowledge you've not left Claddagh in the four weeks you've been here.'

'That could be,' she retorted, 'because I daren't turn my back for fear of what you might get up to in my absence!'

Wilfully he chose to misinterpret her words.

'Afraid I might be unfaithful to you? How very encouraging!'

'You know I meant nothing of the sort.' Noelle spoke without thinking and then cursed herself for rising so easily to the bait. It was several days since he had last suceeded in annoying her, and she saw the instant gleam of satisfaction in his eyes, which prompted her to add, 'And I don't need any shopping. I'd rather stay here, *peacefully*,' she emphasised the word, 'with Aunt Bridie.'

'But then what's sauce for the goose is sauce for the gander,' he returned. 'You don't trust me here alone, neither do I trust you. So go and get ready, there's my good girl.'

Patronising, arrogant, chauvinistic pig, telling her what to do! Noelle fumed as she made her way upstairs to do just that. Despite her protests, her assumed unwillingness to accompany him, in reality she was filled with a nervous, leaping excitement. In his car they would be alone, really alone, whereas here at Claddagh there were always interuptions of one kind or another. If only she and Fergus could get to know each other a little better, might there not be the chance that his dislike and mistrust of her would fade? She had no hope of him ever falling in love with her. What man would who had also seen the gorgeous Suzanne Fahey? But at least liking would be accompanied, she hoped, by respect, and might make him cease the taunts which hurt so much.

The main road into Galway was long and straight, with the mass of the Catholic Cathedral coming into view from a long distance away.

'I'm opening an account at the National Bank,' Fergus told her. 'I'll be transferring all my funds over here, together with the monies from my farm, when it's sold. What about you?'

'I haven't decided anything yet,' she said truthfully. 'I may have to go home for a day or two, talk things over with my uncle. Would it be all right by you if I invited him over for a while? I'd like him to see Claddagh.' Apprehensively she waited for a reply, which, when it came, was surprisingly mild.

'Sure, no problem. I'd like to meet him.'

They parted, Fergus to go to the bank, Noelle to explore, arranging to meet later under the John F. Kennedy monument in Eyre Square.

Noelle's tour of the shops was no idle time-wasting pursuit. She studied carefully just what was available, particullary in the fashion line, and when she went to meet Fergus, it was with a half developed scheme in her head

But other considerations took precedence, when he asked her if she would like to see the old Claddagh part of the town, from which the very first Lord Lissadell had derived his family coat of arms.

To her disappointment there was nothing re-motely romantic about the area nowadays, a grey-walled, dull estate of houses on the west bank of the River Corrib, where once, Fergus told her, there had been single-storey thatched cottages, pictur-esquely and irregularly placed. But its history, as it affected her ancestry, was more interesting.

'The Claddagh used to be an old fishing town. Somewhere about the thirteenth century, Galway was a walled city occupied by the Anglo-Normans, and the native Irish had to live outside the walls. They formed this little town. In the old days the Claddagh never married outside itself, and the Claddagh ring,' he held out his hand indicating the one he wore, 'in the form of two hands clasping a heart, was a traditional heirloom, handed down from mother to daughter. The Lissadells kept up the tradition. This ring was my mother's, and as I have no sisters it came to me. Some day I hope my wife will wear it.'

So Fergus did intend to get married. Despite her misgivings, Noelle had found herself enjoying the afternoon, but now, with plunging spirits, she

wondered if he had anyone particular in mind. It
was a long time since he had repeated his taunt that
he and she ought to marry. She had never taken him
seriously, and now she wished he had meant it.

'Well, whoever she is, I feel sorry for her,' she said
out of her own unhappiness, 'and what happens to
Aunt Bridie when that ever occurs, and to me if it
comes to that? I can't see you wanting us around
once you're married.'

'It could have been you,' he pointed out, his
smile, as always, mocking her, then: 'But I sincerely
hope,' he said, 'that whoever I marry will be capable
of loving and tolerating my aunt for what little time
she has left to her. As to your fate,' he added
somewhat obscurely, 'that's rather up to you.'

'What's that supposed to mean?'

'Let's leave it, Noelle, shall we?' He sounded
irritable now. 'I don't believe in crossing bridges
until I come to them.'

The drive back was accomplished almost in
silence. Noelle had no idea what was occupying
Fergus's thoughts, but for her part she could not
dismiss as lightly as he had the prospect of his
marriage and what it would mean to her.

What had begun as an unwilling fascination,
despite his taunting suspicions of her, had grown
into something deeper, and how could she bear to
stay at Claddagh Hall, or even in Ireland, if he were
to marry? Suddenly she was tinglingly aware of his
nearness, of the occasional brush of his arm as he
changed gear. So acute were her sensations that she
felt her whole body must be giving off electrical
impulses that must surely reach him, alert him to

her quivering desire for him to touch her properly.
She had to get out of the car before she betrayed
herself.

'Stop!' she said, her voice trembling slightly. 'I'd
like to get out. I can walk from here.'

'Travel-sick?' he enquired, but without obeying
her injunction.

'No, I just feel like a walk. You miss a lot of the
countryside whizzing about in cars.'

Immediately he pulled up.

'Right, I don't mind. There's no hurry. We'll both
take a walk.'

'I'd rather go on my own,' she protested, and felt
rather than saw his searching glance.

'We'll both take a walk,' Fergus said decidedly. 'I
think there's something that has to be said, and it
might as well be now as later.' He locked the car,
and, putting his hand through her arm, steered her
off the road and down a lush, grassy slope, over a
low wall and into an area of woodland.

Before them lay a carpet of velvet moss, lined on
both sides by yews of great age, on whose gnarled,
drooping branches the dying afternoon sun cast
shards of light, which, touching the moss, turned it
to the colour of copper. The leaves caught in its rays
were a hundred shades of green.

On the far side of the wood, they came out on to
an eminence from which could be seen the lough,
the sun casting a fiery crimson light across the water
and over the grey walls of Claddagh Hall.

'This is probably the best view of the Hall.'
Fergus threw himself down on the grass, and, after a
second's hesitation, Noelle followed suit, carefully

keeping a distance between them. 'It was Lissadell who first brought me here, and now I come often.'

Against her better judgment, Noelle found herself studying his profile, which now seemed to her to be that of the most attractive man she had ever known. The dying sunlight played tricks with the liberally silvered hair and beard, seemed to soften the ascetic features. As she watched, a smile played about his mouth, relaxing its firm lines.

'I was nearly twelve when old Kelly, Lissadell's solicitor, brought me over to Ireland. He and my mother hadn't spoken for years. She resented his criticism of my father. We'd moved around a lot and when, for some reason, Lissadell decided he wanted to heal the breach, he had no idea where to find us.'

'And your mother, did she come back with you?'

'No.' Fergus was suddenly sober. 'She never came back. She wouldn't come without my father, and she knew he wouldn't be welcome, but she wanted me to see her old home, to know about my Irish roots.' He turned to look at Noelle and she caught her breath, seeing for the first time how those brown eyes could gentle with affection. 'I fell in love with Ireland, with Claddagh, and so long as we managed to keep off the topic of my father, I got on well with Lissadell.'

'Aunt Bridie said you were always rowing?'

'Only latterly, as I got older. After that first visit, I spent every summer holiday in Ireland. The time used to pass too quickly. As soon as I arrived, this was the first place I'd visit and the last place I'd come to before I had to go home.'

He fell silent, and Noelle went on studying his reflective face. She would never have suspected Fergus Carrick of sentimentality.

'You'd really hate to lose it now, wouldn't you?' she said softly. And he wouldn't, if she could help it, she vowed.

He nodded.

'When I was twelve, there was no stud, just the Hall and its farm. In those days Lissadell still hoped that his wife would give him children to inherit the place. But she became more and more of an invalid and gradually he turned his interest to the horses, neglected the house. It was then he and I first began to fall out. I couldn't bear to see what he was doing to Claddagh. It was around then, too, that he came over to England and met your mother.'

'How old were you then?'

'Fourteen when you were born, old enough to be aware of what was going on, but not old enough to understand and forgive him for what he was doing to my Aunt Kathleen.'

'She knew about me?'

'Lissadell told her himself.' Fergus pulled a wry face. 'He wasn't strong enough to bear the weight of his guilt in silence. Besides, at first, he hoped to adopt you. But your mother wouldn't hear of it.'

Now it was Noelle who became thoughtful, but not about her father. Fergus had been fourteen when she was born. That would make him thirty-nine now, the ideal age for a man, she decided. Men of her own age had never held much attraction for her.

But Fergus had mentioned something he wanted

to say to her and she was sure he hadn't brought her here just to talk about his youth. Had he decided, after all, that the subject of his marriage must be broached? She glanced at him uncertainly, and it was as if he guessed her thoughts.

'You're wondering what I really wanted to talk about?' and before she could utter a nervous disclaimer, 'I wanted to talk about us, you and me.'

'Oh?' a little breathlessly. 'I don't see what——'

'Why are you so determined to dislike me?'

It certainly wasn't what she had expected, and for a moment she stared at him blankly, until indignation pierced the haze of her thoughts.

'*Me*, determined to dislike *you*? I'd have said the boot was on the other foot. From the moment you walked into Claddagh, you've done nothing but make insinuations about me, throw my birth up in my face, and then you have the gall to ask me why I——'

'All right, all right!' He placed a placating hand on hers. 'Don't get all steamed up. So maybe we got off on the wrong foot, perhaps I misjudged you——'

'There's no perhaps about it.'

'O.K. So I owe you an apology.' But he hadn't made it, she thought as he went on, 'You asked me once for a truce. It didn't last long, did it? Now I'm asking. Can't we at least be friends, Noelle?'

Her heart beat unevenly as she stared down as though mesmerised by the sight of the hand that rested on hers, a tanned hand with long, sensitive fingers whose flesh seemed to burn where it touched hers. She had an insane longing to know the touch of those fingers on other parts of her body, and it was only with an effort of will that she was able to lift her head and meet his eyes.

'And how long do you think it would last this time?'

'I don't know,' he said frankly, 'but I'd like to try. O.K. by you?'

'I suppose so,' she said slowly, and then as his quick engaging smile lit his face, she felt her own mouth part into an unwilling wavering response. 'But no more cracks about marriages of convenience,' she warned.

'Not another word, ever,' he promised, 'hand on heart.' The readiness of his promise was a little disconcerting. He needn't sound quite so positive, she thought moodily.

'So it's friends then,' he said, 'and as we're cousins, "kissing cousins", I believe the old saying goes, shall we seal the pact?' And before she had had time to take in the full implications of his words, he had pulled her into his arms.

'You're trembling,' he said wonderingly, and at her incoherent little cry, he lowered his head, taking her mouth in a kiss that, whatever its original intent, became something rather more than cousinly.

Noelle gave a strangled gasp in her throat as his hand slid down as though accidentally over her breast, and even though his mouth had freed hers, so that he could explore the column of her throat, for a moment she was quite incapable of finding her voice, then, remembering his enthusiastic agreement not to propose to her again, 'If you want us to stay friends for more than five minutes,' she spat at

him, 'don't do that again!' and she took advantage
of his sudden stillness to pull free, springing to her
feet. 'You can please yourself,' she told him tautly,
'but I'm going home.'

'Home?' he said sharply.

'To Claddagh, of course.' She gave a bitter little
laugh. 'What did you think I meant? Oh no, Fergus,
whatever little tricks you try I'm not running away.'

'You're so right.' Fergus was hard on her heels,
'You're not reneging on our agreement now, just as
I'm beginning to see my way clear to getting
Claddagh out of debt.'

A debt that her help had gone a long way towards
settling! Noelle seethed furiously, as she walked
back to the Hall. She had refused to get back in the
car and to her mingled relief and chagrin, he had
made no attempt to coerce her. After all, why
should he care, she fumed, if she arrived tired, or
stumbled over some obstacle in the rapidly deepen-
ing darkness?

But she had meant what she had said. She wasn't
meekly going to give in and go back to England,
whatever Fergus might try to do or say to annoy her.
She was staying, if only for Bridie O'Rourke's
sake—and that of the house. This attempt at self-
deception was a poor one at best, and Noelle knew
that the fascination Fergus, unknowingly, held for
her, was not so easily denied, that she was unwilling
to leave the field clear for some other woman to
become not only mistress of Claddagh Hall but,
more importantly, Fergus's wife.

In view of her expressed determination not to be

driven away, Noelle decided to postpone her intended trip to London to discuss the future of Noelle et Cie. But since she was anxious to talk over her ideas with John Madox-Browne, she telephoned, asking him if he could spare the time to come to Ireland.

'You're really serious about this?' They were walking in the grounds on his first morning, and Noelle had laid before him the full extent of her plans. As she nodded, 'But why, exactly?'

'That's more difficult to explain. It's just a feeling I've had, right from the first moment I saw Claddagh, that I'd come home.'

'You know you always have a home with me, if you want it.'

'No,' Noelle said gently. 'Oh, I'm not being ungrateful, Uncle John, and I know you mean it, now. But we're not really related and you're still a young man, you may want to marry again some day. My home is here in Ireland, I feel that strongly.'

'But what will the Cohens say about this?'

'I haven't spoken to them yet, but I will, soon. I think they'll jump at the idea.'

'But surely there won't be a market here for the kind of thing Noelle et Cie design?'

'Oh, no. But I think there will be one in Dublin, and one in the provincial towns for original designs based on materials of Irish manufacture, priced for the less affluent pocket. Certainly they should sell to the tourists.'

'You know, I'm sorry,' said John, after they had walked in silence for some time, 'that my procrastination prevented you from meeting your father.'

'Don't be,' Noelle said. 'I've learnt a lot about him since I've been here and I think perhaps it was just as well we didn't meet. He may have been capable of inspiring affection, but I don't believe he was a very admirable man. Look, let's go back now, shall we, and I'll show you just what we plan to do. All those mouldy old hunting trophies are coming down for a start, and we're beginning to redecorate the ground floor. Thank goodness the structure's sound, at least.'

'If you ever need any financial help, don't hesitate to ask.'

'I won't,' affectionately, 'but I don't think it'll be necessary, and remember, I don't want Fergus to know about Noelle et Cie, for the present at least.'

'I can't make up my mind,' John mused as they neared the hall, 'whether you like that young man or not. What *is* your opinion of him?'

Noelle's smile mocked herself.

'My opinion is that he's got a lot of O'Rourke blood in him.'

John's eyes were too shrewd for her liking.

'You mean he too inspires affection? In you? But——'

'Exactly,' she said, '"*but*", and that's something else he need not know.'

They found Miss O'Rourke entertaining a visitor.

'My dear, Miss Fahey has ridden over expressly to see Fergus, but he can't be found.'

He couldn't have known Suzanne was coming over, Noelle brooded darkly, as she introduced the other girl to John, or surely he would have made certain of being available.

'I believe he's gone into Galway. He didn't say when he'd be back,' she added, as Suzanne's lips parted to ask the obvious question.

Suzanne seemed to take a great interest in Noelle and Fergus, in their relation to the late Lord Lissadell and to each other. She also stared with frank curiosity at John. Miss O'Rourke seemed only too delighted to answer the other girl's questions, which to Noelle verged almost on the impertinent. But even she could not help but be disarmed when, as she rose, reluctantly, to leave, Suzanne said with one of her engaging smiles,

'You must all think me terribly nosy, but life round here is so quiet and uneventful. New faces at the Hall are bound to be the object of curiosity. I do hope you'll all come and visit us, and please be as inquisitive as you like about *us*!'

Miss O'Rourke declined the invitation on her own behalf, explaining that her age and increasing infirmities kept her more and more to the house and to early bedtimes.

'But I'm sure the young folk would be delighted.' From her exalted eighty years plus, her glance also embraced John, to her a mere fifty-year-old youth.

'I know!' Suzanne bubbled over with enthusiasm. 'You must come to the party for my parents' ruby wedding anniversary.'

'Surely,' said Noelle, 'they'll want that to be family only?'

'What family?' Suzanne laughed. 'There's only the three of us—and they don't even know they're having a party. I've only just thought of it!'

General laughter followed this remark, and Noelle asked, 'So when is it to be?'

'Saturday,' which was in three days' time, 'and you will *all* come, all three of you?' Suzanne insisted.

As she accepted for herself and John, Noelle reflected wryly that it was unlikely she would have to do much pressurising where Fergus was concerned.

'Yes, I'm sure we'll all be there.'

'A charming girl,' commented John when their visitor had departed.

'Fergus certainly seems to think so,' Noelle returned, and was incensed when her unwary retort caused Miss O'Rourke and her uncle to exchange amused glances.

As Noelle had surmised, Fergus was only too willing to attend the social gathering at the Faheys.

'I suppose a present will be in order?'

Noelle had been thinking along the same lines.

'It's awkward though, not knowing them very well. We don't want to embarrass them.' She suspected too that Fergus's finances would not run to anything very expensive, and in view of her own reticence to date, she couldn't very well offer to bear the cost.

John Madox-Browne resolved the difficulty.

'Suppose you let me take care of it, for all three of us, as my return for Claddagh's hospitality?'

John's taste was impeccable. On their arrival, he presented Mrs Fahey with a superb bouquet of forty red roses, and to her husband he gave a bottle of whiskey. Somehow he had discovered their host's favourite brand.

'And it didn't seem fair to neglect the organiser of this event,' he told Suzanne gravely, presenting her with a posy of sweet-smelling violets that echoed the colour of the girl's eyes.

Noelle was a trifle dismayed, and Fergus quite evidently annoyed, to find Patrick Byrne also one of the twenty guests present. As well as disliking the other man for his pretensions to Claddagh, did Fergus also see him as a serious contender for Suzanne? Certainly the other girl had her work cut out to keep both men amused at the dinner table. Seated on either side of her, each demanded her conversational attention, continually interrupting each other. Noelle, on Fergus's other side, soon gave up any attempt to compete and concentrated on Mr Fahey who sat next to her.

'Bonny girl, our Suzanne,' he said fondly, 'don't you think so, Miss Madox-Browne?'

'Please call me Noelle. Yes, she is very attractive.'

'A better daughter a man couldn't ask for, since the Lord saw fit not to give me sons.' Terence Fahey seemed not to require any answer, happy to embark on a monologue of praise. 'Well, everything I have will be hers some day, and believe me, she deserves it. I just wish,' he added wistfully, 'that she would settle down and raise me some grandchildren. The wife and I aren't getting any younger, and frankly, neither is Suzanne. If she leaves it much longer, it'll be too late.'

It seemed probable to Noelle that the Faheys had set their sights on one or other of the two men seated either side of their daughter. But which would they prefer as a son-in-law? Patrick Byrne had the money, Fergus had the property. Did it matter about money though, so long as the desired grandchildren were forthcoming? Especially since all Terence Fahey's money and property would be his daughter's some day. Already it was apparent that he made her a generous allowance. The Grecian-style white gown she wore tonight had cost a pretty penny, but it was cash well invested, judging by the admiring glances her superbly voluptuous figure was drawing from all the men present.

Noelle, it was true, had taken some pains over her own appearance, and her dress, a delicate web of hand-crochet, in a subtle lilac, clung softly to her slight, gently curved body. But though her mirror had told her she looked her best, she didn't suppose anyone having seen Suzanne would give her a second glance.

After dinner, however, as the guests circulated more freely, Noelle found Patrick Byrne at her side, and a swiftly comprehensive glance revealed to her the undoubted reason for his attentions. Fergus had finally succeeded in monopolising Suzanne. They were presently occupying a settee built to accommodate only two persons, and their heads were together in close conversation. The stab of jealousy Noelle felt at this discovery made her more than normally responsive to Patrick, and she made sure that any onlooker would be in no doubt how much she was enjoying his company.

Certainly Patrick himself seemed much encouraged by this display, and towards the end of the evening, when Suzanne and Fergus seemed to have disappeared, Patrick asked if he might see her home.

It was then Noelle realised how rashly she had been behaving. Trying to create a false impression for one man, she had succeeded all too well in deluding another. She looked around her, hoping to make the need to accompany her uncle her excuse. But he too was nowhere to be seen. To refuse now would seem a totally illogical reversal of her friendly manner towards him since their first meeting. Putting a good face on things, she accepted his offer of a lift.

As if to point up his wealth, Patrick ran a needlessly large and opulent car. On the country lanes around Claddagh, Noelle doubted if he ever got it into top gear.

'Fergus Carrick seems to get on well with Suzanne,' he commented as they drove away, and Noelle wondered if Patrick had serious hopes himself in that direction. But his next remark made her realise that if such had been the case, Patrick had made a speedy adjustment. 'But he's welcome to the little heiress, for I don't doubt her father's money would be welcome. Personally, I prefer brunettes.' His smiling glance at Noelle was meant to leave her in no doubt of which brunette he favoured, and as she deliberately made no reply, he asked, 'You do like me, Noelle?'

'Yes, of course,' she said in matter-of-fact tones,

'after all, we're related, aren't we?'

Patrick smiled a little wryly.

'Actually, the two things have no logical connection. Sometimes mere acquaintances are preferable to our relations. But,' he paused, 'we could be making the relationship an even closer one. I'd be willing if you were?'

Purposely Noelle feigned incomprehension, which was a mistake. She should have discouraged him politely, but immediately, she realised. For now he braked, steering the car on to the side of the road, flicked on the interior light and turned to look at her.

'I mean I'd like to marry you, Noelle. I realise we haven't known each other very long, but time is unimportant in love, isn't it?'

Was Patrick in love with her? she wondered cynically, and doubted it. Like Fergus, he was probably only interested in what she represented, a half share in Claddagh. Her suspicions were not unfounded evidently, for unwisely he added:

'I could well afford to buy Fergus Carrick's half of Claddagh. I doubt he'd want to share a house with me, and you'd rather own the whole than a part of it, wouldn't you?'

Would she? Forgetting that Patrick, presumably, required some kind of answer, Noelle fell into a brown study. She had many times rejected the idea of leaving Claddagh Hall, leaving Fergus in sole possession. Her taunts that he could always buy her out had been safely uttered. Fergus couldn't afford it. But what if the positions were reversed? Suppose she had total ownership and Fergus were the one to leave?

Intolerable! Much as she loved Claddagh, it wouldn't be the same without him. At last she had to face the facts. Her squabbles with Fergus, her distrust of him, of his motives for proposing friendship, had merely been a smokescreen erected in an attempt to hide the truth from herself, a truth reinforced by the strong physical awareness of him which she had recognised from their very first encounter, and by her recently acquired jealousy of Suzanne. She was in love with Fergus, and swift exaltation of spirits plunged as rapidly into despair. *He* didn't love *her*.

CHAPTER SIX

'NOELLE? You're very quiet all of a sudden. Are you angry with me?'

With a start, she returned to more immediate problems.

'Sorry, Patrick! Of course I'm not annoyed. I'm very flattered—but the answer has to be no. Even if I felt we'd known each other long enough, I——'

'Of course!' At once Patrick was all apologies. 'I've spoken too soon, impetuous idiot that I am. Forget I spoke, right? We'll get to know each other better first?'

'Patrick, please believe me, it's no use. I . . .'

'There's someone else?'

'No. I . . . that is . . .'

'Sure and there has to be, or you'd at least be willing to give me a chance. Is it this Englishman you've brought over?'

John's full name and his exact relationship to Noelle had not been mentioned in front of Patrick, she realised, and if she did explain, the next candidate for his suspicions would be Fergus. Then it might be difficult for her to make a convincing denial, and if he suspected the truth, it would only add fuel to his already flaring hostility against his cousin.

'I'm very fond of John, of course,' she began, feeling her way, intending to go on 'though not in

104

that way', but her first words were sufficient for Patrick, secure in his own self-confidence.

'Sure and if that's all, I'll undertake to make you more than fond of me.'

Before she could forestall him, he had reached out for her and started kissing her. It wasn't exactly an unpleasant experience, Noelle thought judicially, but there was no magic in the touch of his lips on hers. If there had been, she wouldn't have been able to set herself so apart from the sensation and analyse it, comparing his kisses unfavourably with those of Fergus, aware too all the time of extraneous sounds such as those of passing cars. As soon as she was able without an undignified struggle, she pulled away.

'It's no good, Patrick,' she said calmly. 'I like you very much as a person, as a cousin, but——'

'As a cousin, by all the saints!' With a sound of exasperation he put the car into gear and the powerful machine surged forward, its wheels spinning noisily on the loose surface of the road. For a few moments Noelle was actually afraid, but then Patrick seemed to recollect himself, see the potential danger in which he placed them, and by the time he pulled up on the forecourt of Claddagh Hall, he had himself once more under control.

'Thank you for the lift,' said Noelle, and then, awkwardly, 'I'm sorry, Patrick, really I am, but——'

'Will you remember now,' he interrupted, laying a detaining hand on her arm, 'our being cousins makes no odds at all. Your marrying me would be no different from your marrying Carrick. The relationship's the same, and besides, we outcasts ought to stick together!'

The front door, Noelle realised to her annoyance, was firmly shut and locked, and she had no key. Bother Fergus! He must have got home ahead of her. It was only since his arrival that such precautions had been insisted on. She was pretty certain, too, that it would be of no use trying rear and side doors.

Well, if Fergus wanted doors locked, he must put up with the inconvenience of being woken, for his bedroom was the only one that overlooked the front of the house—the master suite, Miss O'Rourke called it, and Fergus certainly seemed to think he was master here! It grated on Noelle whenever she made a request to one of the servants or the outdoor staff, invariably to receive the reply 'Does the master know about that, then?' That was male-orientated Ireland for you.

Grasping the huge door knocker in both hands, she pounded it persistently. Far sooner than she had expected, the door was flung open, and since she still grasped the brass fox's head, she was dragged with it, stumbling a little. She would have fallen but for Fergus's grasp on her arm, which seemed unnecessarily prolonged.

'Trying to wake all our ancestors?' he asked crisply.

'No,' she retorted, nerves screaming at his proximity, 'just one pig-headed descendant. If you weren't so paranoid about locked doors, I wouldn't have had to waken you.'

'You didn't,' he said calmly. 'I was waiting up.'

'There was no need for that. If you'd left the door——'

'There was every need,' he began.

'Why?' she demanded, without allowing him to finish. 'Just because I was out there somewhere with Patrick? You don't have to constitute yourself as my guardian, you know!'

'I've no desire whatsoever to be your guardian, believe me!' Fergus retorted. 'You're obviously stubbornly determined to go your own way in spite of any warnings I——'

'If you mean that I'm determined to remain on good terms with my cousin——'

'It seems to me you're on *very* good terms! But it might be as well, in future, to advise Byrne not to leave on the interior light of his car, especially in moments of passion.'

Noelle remembered the sound of passing cars and flushed. One of those cars had been Fergus's.

'You saw us, so what? I've nothing to be ashamed of, and if you waited up just to lecture me again . . .?'

'I waited up,' he said repressively, 'because I'm expecting the doctor to call at any moment. Aunt Bridie isn't at all well.'

At once their dispute was forgotten, as Noelle's eyes widened, cheeks regained their normal hue, her features drawing into anxious lines.

'What's wrong? How bad is it? Can I see her?

'Siobhan is with her, but you can go up, certainly. As a matter of fact she's been asking for you.'

'And I wasn't here!' Noelle berated herself as she

made for the upper landing.

Miss O'Rourke was lying down, still fully dressed, her face chalk-white against her rose-hued pillows. Her manner was more than a little *distraite*, and far from seeking Noelle's presence, she seemed not to notice her arrival.

'How is she, Siobhan? What happened?' Noelle whispered to the elderly general factotum.

'Well, miss, I found herself walking around downstairs. Very strange she seemed, to be sure. She was looking for himself . . .'

'For Fergus?'

'Oh no, miss, his late Lordship.'

Noelle bent over Miss O'Rourke.

'Aunt Bridie, it's me, Noelle. How are you feeling?'

The old lady's eyes seemed to look through and beyond her, and Noelle had to lean close to hear the words distorted by her slurred speech.

'Nonsense! Noel is a man. Where is he? I can't find him. I must talk to him about the will.'

'Wandering in her wits,' old Siobhan said with gloomy relish.

Fortunately, at that moment, Fergus ushered the doctor into the room and Noelle joined him outside on the landing, leaving the elderly servant to attend her mistress. Noelle looked up at Fergus.

'Has she ever been like this before?'

'Apparently she had a stroke about a year ago. I wasn't here at the time, but I understand she made a swift and complete recovery.' Suddenly his arm went around Noelle's shoulders and he drew her to him. 'Don't look so stricken. She's a very old lady.

We can't keep her for ever.'

'No,' Noelle admitted on a sobbing breath. 'But
she can't die yet—not yet, please God, not just as
I've got to know her and love her. And she still
enjoys life so much.'

Fergus continued to hold her, and as if it were the
most natural thing in the world that she should do
so, she turned her face against his chest, her arms
going about his waist as she sought comfort from his
warmth and strength.

'Noelle,' he said after a while, his voice sounding
husky, unlike his normal clear, ringing tones. 'I
think the doctor's about finished. Maybe we
should . . .'

She drew away from him and turned towards the
bedroom door, waiting tensely for it to open, but
some of the new courage Fergus's nearness had
given her lingered, and she watched with at least
outward composure as the doctor emerged, then
beckoned to them to follow him into the adjoining
sitting room. Side by side they face him, all their
recent differences forgotten in one common cause.

'She's a very old lady,' the doctor began,
unknowingly echoing Fergus's words. 'But I think
she'll pull through this time. She seems to be
troubled about something. It's important,' he said
almost severely, 'that she has no undue stress placed
upon her.' He handed Fergus a slip of paper. 'I've
left some tablets with Siobhan for now. First thing,
get this prescription made up. I'll look in again
myself some time tomorrow, or today, I should
say——' He consulted an old-fashioned fob watch.

'You'd better get some rest,' Fergus said gruffly a

few minutes later as he looked at Noelle's small, tired features. 'We'll have to share the nursing with Siobhan until—if—Aunt Bridie gets back on her feet again.'

Noelle nodded, her face working convulsively.

'Fergus, do you think we could have made her ill, with our constant arguing?'

Gravely he considered her question, then spread his hands in a gesture of defeat.

'I honestly don't know, though I wouldn't have thought so. The O'Rourkes have always been a noisy, quarrelsome family and usually she takes it all in her stride. But perhaps,' he hesitated, 'perhaps we might try a little harder, hmm?' He stretched out a hand and lifted Noelle's chin. 'Well?'

She felt a sudden shyness invade her and her eyelids dropped before his penetrating stare.

'I'm willing if you are.'

'Shall we shake on it?' he asked, offering his hand, then, teasingly, 'Since you seem to object so strongly to being kissed, at least by me.'

To her amazement, Noelle heard her own voice, which sounded almost like that of a stranger, saying, 'You . . . you can kiss me if you like—just,' her more rational self added hastily, 'just as a token of goodwill.' She looked up to gauge his reaction and found herself unable to look away.

Fergus regarded her long and steadily, before he reached out and placed a hand on either of her shoulders.

'Sure?' he said quietly.

Mutely she nodded and raised her face as he pulled her closer, letting herself relax completely against him. The touch of his lips on hers was gentle, warm, very slightly moist, as though his tongue had just passed over them, and Noelle could not be sure through which one of them the shudder ran. Then he was putting her away from him.

'So we're agreed. Whatever we may think privately of each other, outwardly we'll appear to be the best of friends?'

Again she nodded, once more unable to speak. She wished he hadn't put it quite that way. It lent an air of insincerity to a *rapprochement* which on her side at least was completely genuine. She was tired of fighting with Fergus. What had been half in fun at first, stimulating, a slightly dangerous flirting, had palled. She longed instead for a peaceful co-existence, and more than that.

Upstairs, waiting outside Bridie O'Rourke's bedroom for the doctor's verdict, she had known, in Fergus's arms, a deep sense of security, of belonging. That must be what it felt like to be loved.

'Go to bed, little Noelle!' Fergus's voice was tender, but as if, she thought miserably, he spoke to a child. She turned and left him, aware now of just how tired she was, not only physically but with a weariness of the emotions.

But tomorrow was a new day, she told herself in an attempt to lighten her spirits. She would fight again, this time for a different goal, not against Fergus, but for him, in an attempt to gain his genuine friendship, his liking, even if she couldn't have his love.

During the night, Miss O'Rourke had a second

stroke, so the doctor confirmed when he called back. This time it had rendered her totally speechless and had affected her right hand. She might, in time, the doctor thought, recover from these disabilities. She had done so on a previous occasion.

Since there was illness in the house, John Madox-Browne cut short his visit, despite a cordial invitation from the Faheys to accommodate him for his remaining time, and he left for England.

In the next few days, Noelle spent hours at her great-aunt's bedside, attending to her needs and anxiously waiting for the return of recognition in the faded eyes. When it did return Noelle was present, but she could not rejoice as she might have done, for without speech the eyes became anguished, unable to impart their message.

'There's something she wants to say, I know it,' she told Fergus in a tremulous whisper. 'It must be awful, so frustrating.' She was close to tears and he looked at her consideringly.

'You really do care, but you're looking pale yourself. You've been spending too much time cooped up in here. You need some recreation time. I'm going to ask Dr Cadogan to send in a nurse.'

'Oh no, that's not necessary. I'd rather stay here. Siobhan and I can manage between us.'

'You can't! If it were just for a short period of time I might agree, but we've no idea how long it will be till she recovers—if ever,' he added as he steered Noelle through the doorway. His own anxiety harshened his voice. 'Siobhan's getting on in years herself, and you'll be no use to Aunt Bridie or to anyone else if you crack up too. You look dreadful, Noelle.' He sounded angry. 'Go out this minute, now, into the grounds and get some fresh air, and don't argue!'

Worry and lack of sleep had played havoc with her appearance, Noelle knew, and not only her looks had suffered, but her nerves. Fergus's comments on her wan appearance, his brusque command, was the last straw, and in her over-tired, irrational state it sounded hard and unfeeling. He was concerned, not for her, but because if she were to become ill he would have another invalid on his hands. Averting her face so he could not see the weak, silly tears that trickled down her pale cheeks, she hurried from the room.

Outside even the weather reflected her mood, as a soft rain fell, obscuring the mountain tops and the waters of the lough. It was hardly walking weather, but Fergus had ordered her to walk and she would walk. She set off with no particular destination in mind. But, lost as she was in her thoughts and worries, her feet automatically trod a path they had followed many times before, until she found herself in the vicinity of Patrick's cottage.

She would have passed by, she was in no mood for socialising, but he had seen her from his window and called to her to come in and take shelter.

'What on earth? You'll be taking a chill, walking in this weather and with no coat on.'

Absently, Noelle looked down at herself. It was true. In her haste she had gone out just as she was, in a skirt and blouse, the soft material of which now clung damply to her body.

Patrick fetched a towel and his own dressing gown, suggesting that she remove her wet things, turning his back while she did so.

Clad in Patrick's robe, she sat and towelled her hair, while on the back of a chair her clothes steamed before the peat fire which Patrick kept continually burning.

'I haven't seen you for days,' he complained. 'Is it true what they say, that Miss O'Rourke is dying?'

'No!' Noelle began fiercely. 'She *is not*! She's going to get better. She has to . . .' Her voice broke and in an instant Patrick was at her side, taking her in his arms. 'There now, *alannah*, don't upset yourself.'

Too proud to lower her defences before Fergus, Noelle laid her head on Patrick's shoulder and cried.

It occurred to Fergus, after Noelle had left their great-aunt's bedroom so precipitately, that he hadn't expressed himself very tactfully. Noelle might well be forgiven for thinking that he didn't care a jot about her health so long as no one else was inconvenienced. He pushed one of the old-fashioned bells with which the Hall abounded and waited impatiently until Siobhan, short of breath, answered its summons.

'Would you stay with my aunt for a while, until I get back?'

A visit to Noelle's room assured him she wasn't there. She must have taken his advice, issued more like a command, he ruefully acknowledged, and gone outside. A swift search of the immediate environs of house and outbuildings also proved fruitless, and he paused for thought. Where would she be most likely to go, and in this miserable weather, a soft day, native-born Irishmen would call it, while he could think of less flattering descriptions.

He had a guilty suspicion that Noelle had been more than a little upset when she had left, even though she had averted her face. To whom would she be likely to turn for comfort? Beneath his beard his jaw set grimly as the answer came to him. If she went to anyone, it would be to Patrick Byrne.

But in case he was wrong, he whistled up the wolfhounds, who could be relied upon to find her. He smiled a little to himself. It was ironic, because Noelle still held aloof from them, yet Cleo and Caesar were ready to adore the girl.

The animals at his heels, he stepped out across the rain-misted fields towards the cottage by the lough. As he drew nearer, he could see that someone had switched on a light against the greyness of the day outside and the smoke curling limply down over the roof spoke of a peat fire burning.

Fergus had no wish to call on Patrick Byrne, or to be seen by him, and he avoided the front door, making a detour that would take him past the lighted window. At the sight that met his outraged eyes, he stopped in his tracks, the dogs barking and looking up at him enquiringly at this interruption to their unexpected walk.

In full view, Noelle stood enfolded in Patrick's arms, her dark head nestled against his shoulder. And what the hell, Fergus wondered, was she

wearing? It looked like a man's dressing gown.
Surely she hadn't . . . but as Fergus stared, Patrick,
perhaps alerted by the dogs' noise, looked out and
met his cousin's eyes. At once his face broke into a
smile of triumphant satisfaction.

Patrick's embrace was meant to be comforting,
Noelle knew, and for a moment it was good to rest
on someone else's strength. But his arms couldn't
compare with Fergus's, and she was aware after a
while of a restlessness in him. Belatedly she realised
that holding her in his arms was disturbing him.
Quickly she pulled free, dashing a hand across her
eyes.

'Sorry, Patrick. I'm not normally the weepy type.'
Then she noticed that his eyes were fixed on
something beyond the window, his expression
almost a smirk. She followed his gaze and groaned
inwardly as she too recognised the tall retreating
figure with its grey attendants. She had no doubt
that Fergus had seen her in Patrick's arms.

She could guess what he must be thinking, that
she had taken advantage of his freeing her from the
sickroom only to rush to Patrick, to indulge in a
little lovemaking. She could imagine exactly how
his mind would be working. And why had he come
after her? Was Bridie O'Rourke worse? But surely
in that case even his dislike of Patrick wouldn't
have prevented him knocking on the door? But she
didn't know him well enough to be certain.

'I must go back,' she said, her voice rising on a
note of panic.

'But your clothes aren't ready yet.'

'It doesn't matter. They'll only get wet again. I must get back, in case ... I think Fergus was looking for me ... Aunt Bridie might ...'

He nodded understandingly.

'Then I'll take you back in the car. Quicker than walking—drier, too.'

He shot her a curious glance as they took the roadway that ran alongside the lough, then circled back on itself to reach the Hall.

'You're really fond of that old woman, aren't you? I wish you were half as fond of me. Noelle ...?'

'Please, Patrick,' she pleaded, 'not now.'

'All right,' he agreed, then with a triumphant note in his voice, 'But I'll not be forgetting that it was me you came to in your trouble, not Fergus Carrick.' He braked at the bottom of the front steps and, seeing Fergus in the doorway, deliberately leant across, holding Noelle's shoulders so that he could kiss her full on the mouth. 'I'll not be forgetting,' he repeated as he released her, and for a moment he sat there, watching her mount the steps to be greeted by Fergus with what looked like angry gestures and expostulations. He wasn't far wrong.

'When I suggested you needed some recreation, I didn't mean of that kind,' Fergus said as soon as Noelle was within earshot. 'You didn't waste much time, did you, or was the dressing gown before and not after?'

Noelle was no longer feeling tearful, and it was a blazing anger instead that illumined her eyes, making their blue darker and deeper, as she paused halfway up the main staircase.

'That's not the first time you've spied on me,' she

accused him over the banister rail. 'Where I go and what I do is none of your business. I thought something was wrong, but instead ... How dare you follow me and——'

'I *dared*, as you call it,' he returned, his voice deepened and thickened by anger, as he mounted the stairs towards her, 'because, perhaps belatedly, I realised I'd upset you. I wanted to apologise, to see if you were all right. Well, I soon found that you were very much all right, that you didn't need *me*.'

Noelle stared at him, the angry brilliance fading from her eyes. But she *had* needed him, so much. Patrick hadn't even been a poor second best.

'At least Patrick showed a bit of sympathy,' she said wearily, 'which is more than I ever get from you. And when I saw you, outside the cottage, I thought Aunt Bridie was worse ...'

'But your anxiety didn't prevent you indulging in a final amorous embrace in front of me, did it?'

'It wasn't ... *I* wasn't,' she began, but indignation could carry her through no further and her voice faltered. 'Is she all right? Oh, Fergus, don't, please don't quarrel with me right now. I ... I don't think I can bear any more.'

Unexpectedly, during her speech, his manner had altered.

'She's no worse, you poor little scrap. Why, there's nothing of you really, is there? I forget that when you're in one of your towering rages. But you're not always such a firebrand after all, it seems. I suppose it was my fault that you were driven to Byrne's arms for comfort! Come here!'

She nodded wordlessly and went unprotestingly

into his arms as they closed about her, lifted her up and carried her the rest of the way to the landing and on, into her room. She was so tired, drained of all emotion, she thought.

He stood by the bed, still holding her, looking down into her eyes which slowly widened and deepened under his gaze. As she began to tremble, gently he set her down.

None of their previous encounters had gone beyond a kiss, a tentative caress, but the look in his eyes, the pulse beating in his temple, were indicative of an involuntary arousal, and she felt an impotent weakness engulf her. His name broke from her lips. The single sound embodied all her desires, her doubts, the confusion between the two.

He bent over her, and her body throbbed to his nearness, a sweet, painful longing. He put out a tentative, exploratory hand, stroking her hair as if to gentle her into acquiescence, let the silky strands run lingeringly through his fingers.

'Noelle?' He said her name on a rising, wondering inflection and for a few seconds something intangible, indefinable, passed between them.

But then, just as it seemed he would lean closer, the sound of hurrying feet, their names being called, roused them from their bemusement with one another.

'Mr Fergus! Miss Noelle!' It was Siobhan, her voice rising hysterically.

The thought occurred to them simultaneously, 'Aunt Bridie!' and Noelle, released from mesmerism, moved swiftly, so that they reached the door together.

'What is it?' It was Fergus who found voice to rap out the question that plagued them both, while Noelle stood, a hand apprehensively at her throat.

''Tis herself, Mr Fergus! Saints be praised! Didn't she just move her hand?'

Again they moved as one, to Bridie O'Rourke's bedside, not daring to believe until they had seen for themselves. There was dawning hope now in the faded eyes that met theirs, and Bridie's hand, which had caused Siobhan's excitement, curled around Noelle's fingers.

'Dear Aunt Bridie!' she exclaimed. 'You'll soon be well now, won't she, Fergus?'

His arm rested about her shoulders as he gave the affirmative, and it seemed to Noelle that her great-aunt's mouth curved slightly at the sight of the two of them so close together. And as Fergus gently urged Noelle away, once more it seemed right that his arm should remain about her.

He walked her back to her room. On its threshold he looked down at her, and it seemed to Noelle that there was an enquiry in the brown eyes, a stillness between them as of a storm of feeling about to break. But perhaps it was just her own awareness of him?

'Noelle?'

'Fergus!'

They spoke together and he motioned her to proceed.

'Ladies first!'

'I just wanted to ask, to know,' she said wistfully, 'if you still feel the same way about me as ... as when we first met, I mean?'

He was a long time answering her question, his eyes consideringly upon her face. Then, his own an inscrutable mask, he said, 'Exactly the same. I generally find first impressions stand me in good stead. But I like to test them out, nevertheless.'

'Oh!' It was said in a very small, doubtful voice. The emotional upheavals of the last hour or two had left Noelle very vulnerable, and she had to swallow, hard, as she wondered just what Fergus was finding so amusing.

'Goodnight, Noelle.' He said it gently. 'It's been a long day.' Then, as she made no move, her eyes still questioningly on his face, he muttered something she couldn't hear and caught her to him, his mouth kissing hers gently, teasingly, until a wild compulsion made her respond.

As the touch of his lips seemed to fuse every nerve in her body, her hands slid up to lose themselves in his hair, and the slightly coarser texture of his beard seemed to impart a greater sensuality to his kiss, sending needle-like sensations of excitement through her quivering body.

How wonderful it would be to be utterly possessed by him, totally loved. But what was she thinking of? Fergus had made it clear that his first impressions of her were unaltered. Desperately she fought back the urgent needs of her body and dragged herself free, shaking her head in a frenzied negation of all that her responses had seemed to promise.

'Now what?' It was half amusement, half exasperation, but he made no attempt to restrain her.

'You were right. It's late and I'm tired,' she said, striving for normality of voice. 'And we don't need to carry your truce that far. There's no one to see us here.'

Their moment of physical rapport, brief as it had been, left Noelle with heightened emotions, the knowledge that it had only served to intensify her feelings towards Fergus, whereas he ... Just what had Fergus's behaviour conveyed? That sexually she was not unattractive to him? A moment of euphoria that the anxiety they had shared was lessened? On her side it had been a moment of weakness, when she had succumbed to her love for Fergus, whereas on his it could have been nothing but the passing sensual needs of a virile male, aroused by her uncharacteristic weakness. Certainly his only response to her words had been a shrug of the shoulders, which seemed to convey total indifference, even if the expression in his eyes had been unfathomable.

She was nervous of facing him next morning, afraid that he might make some reference to that moment in her doorway. Despite their so-called truce, she sensed that he enjoyed deliberately provoking her. At such times the brown eyes had a certain gleam, especially when she couldn't help rising to his tormenting insinuations. But his manner towards her gave no sign that he even remembered the incident.

As Miss O'Rourke's health steadily improved, Noelle knew she could no longer delay her promised visit to London for business discussions with the

Cohens. Despite her promise that she would return at the earliest possible moment, her great-aunt bade her a somewhat tearful farewell. She could not gauge Fergus's reactions to her leaving, though he was certainly curious about the reasons for it.

'Why go all the way to England just to hand in your notice? I assume that is your intention? Surely a letter would have been sufficient,' he said, as he drove her to the airport.

'You don't understand. It's not that simple,' she fenced, 'and I should feel discourteous. You'll look after Aunt Bridie, won't you?' she said anxiously as he left her in the departure lounge.

He didn't linger, and as he strode away, her eyes followed him hungrily. It would seem strange after all these weeks not to see him every day, not to know exactly where he was, what he was doing. Would he be seeing Suzanne? The serpent of jealousy coiled and struck without warning. While Miss O'Rourke had been ill, their socialising had, of necessity, been curtailed, but with his aunt so much better, Fergus would be free to come and go as he chose now.

After the leisurely Irish life style, England— London itself—seemed noisier, more hurried than Noelle remembered. The city's varied colours jarred on eyes accustomed to endless soft greens and browns, the golden gorse, the purple of heather. The Cohens greeted her rapturously, and to her considerable relief approved her ideas for expansion.

'This way we don't lose you altogether,' Rachel Cohen said practically, 'and we get more business.'

Noelle accompanied her partners on a tour of the workrooms and salons and noticed with some amusement that the paintings brought over from Ireland had been professionally cleaned. The fastidious Rachel, she guessed as she remarked on them.

'Clients are always asking if they're for sale,' Rachel told her, 'but I've been waiting to consult you.'

Noelle shrugged. The works didn't appeal to her particularly.

'If someone offers you more than I paid, fine, sell them.' And she promptly forgot the matter.

A flying visit to John, giving him news of all those back in Galway, and then she was on her way to Ireland once more, with an uplifting sensation of homecoming. She had advised Fergus of her E.T.A., and it was a strong disappointment to find that he hadn't come to meet her himself, but had instead despatched one of the stable lads.

'I suppose Mr Carrick was too busy?' she asked casually as they drove, and her driver nodded enthusiastically.

'Sure and isn't he the lucky one, away to the Curragh this day, with Miss Suzanne, to the races.'

Noelle wished at once that she hadn't asked, certain that the reason for her sudden silence would be obvious to the man.

She tried to disguise her pain with inconsequential chatter about the weather, the lush, fertile state of the countryside through which they passed.

For a while she was able to dull the edges of her hurt in Bridie O'Rourke's relieved welcome, her demand to know everything Noelle had seen and done during her brief absence.

'Everything's settled,' Noelle told her. 'Except for the occasional business trip to London, I'm here permanently.' Unless, to herself she added the rider, unless Fergus were to marry Suzanne, in which case he would be well able to buy Noelle out. But she preferred not to dwell on that possibility, which would mean the loss of everything she now held dear—and the Hall was now the least of her concerns.

However, she was to be reminded of the subject when Fergus, returning from the Curragh, brought Suzanne to see Miss O'Rourke, both of them with glowing reports of their day out, and the other girl was invited to stay and share their evening meal.

'He's been out with Suzanne once or twice while you've been away,' Bridie O'Rourke told Noelle later, when they were alone. She sounded concerned, Noelle thought. 'I had hoped that you and Fergus would fall in love. It would have been so suitable and very convenient for everyone. But if you don't . . .' Her worried frown deepened and she left her sentence unfinished, so that Noelle wondered if this last stroke had left her great-aunt a little absent-minded.

She had looked forward so much to coming back to Claddagh Hall, to seeing Fergus again, that it came as an unpleasant surprise to find that he too intended going away, for at least a week.

'I can leave with a clear conscience now you're here to look after Aunt Bridie,' he told her.

'You, of course, sat with her all day, every day

while I was away?' she said sarcastically, but to her chagrin, she could not annoy him in the way he could so easily annoy her.

'No,' he replied equably, 'I don't think you'll find that's necessary. Aunt Bridie will probably encourage you, as she did me, to get out and about.'

'And you certainly took her at her word!'

His response was a mocking smile and the question, 'Shall you miss me, while I'm away, Noelle?'

'Did *you* miss *me*?' she returned, evading the issue.

'The house was certainly more peaceful.' He could be evasive too.

'Well, that's how it'll be when you're gone,' she wasted no time in informing him, adding, though it was far from what she felt, 'so don't hurry back!'

'Oh, we won't,' he assured her. 'I don't believe I mentioned it, but Suzanne is coming with me, and since she's never been to England we'll probably fit in a little sightseeing.'

CHAPTER SEVEN

IT lessened Noelle's shock a little when she found that both Terence and Maeve Fahey would also be going on the trip to England, but even so, the whole notion lent so much credence to the idea of an understanding between Fergus and Suzanne that this fact wasn't much comfort.

Despite Noelle's insinuation that Fergus wouldn't be missed, he was, very much so, both by her and by her great-aunt. Although Miss O'Rourke, perhaps a little frailer than of yore, was much recovered, there was a restlessness, an uneasiness about her that Noelle seemed not to remember. Of course, being in her eighties, this most recent reminder of her own mortality must have been very alarming, yet to Noelle, questioning her in a roundabout way, she professed not to fear death. So what was worrying Bridie O'Rourke?

Noelle, meanwhile, busied herself with the redecoration of the Hall, and with her facility for draping material to good effect upon living models she discovered an equal talent for re-upholstery, so that the ground floor at least was beginning to look more cared-for, more homelike.

But even Noelle had her limitations where a capacity for sheer hard work was involved, and one morning, feeling sorely in need of relaxation, she wandered down towards the lough. It was safe enough to take that direction today. Patrick was away too, visiting relations of his late mother. Although firmly fixed in her determination that Patrick was entitled to recognition and civility from the 'big house', as he mockingly called it, Noelle wasn't anxious to encourage a repetition of his attentions towards herself.

En route to the lough, she found herself being shadowed by Caesar and Cleo, and though she had by now accepted Fergus's assurance that the great dogs would not harm her, she was still uneasy in their presence. Childhood fears died hard.

At the edge of the lough, the Claddagh property boasted its own stone harbour, once an elegant adornment, now crumbling and moss-grown. But it was still in use, mainly by Patrick on his fishing expeditions, she gathered, and two small rowing boats were tied alongside the steps. In her teens, Noelle had been fond of rowing, and she was suddenly curious to see whether she still retained the skill. A brisk little breeze was stirring the surface of the water as she stepped into one of the boats and set the oars in their rowlocks, but the seemingly ever-present rainclouds were high and scattered.

The lough, Fergus had told her, was around twenty-seven miles long and, except in the northern part, nowhere over twenty feet deep. But Noelle could swim reasonably well and did not intend to venture any further than the nearest of the innumerable small islets.

She was somewhat concerned to see that the wolfhounds had taken to the water, following in her wake, but as they seemed to be strong swimmers and in no danger, she forgot about them and bent to her task.

Rowing was a little harder than she remembered, but she hadn't lost its rhythm and co-ordination and, albeit with reddening hands and aching arms, she reached her goal after half an hour's steady progress.

Once, this island had probably been a favourite target for the more water-loving amongst the Lissadell family, for it too boasted a small brown-stone quay, though suitable only for fair weather mooring. The island itself, however, was sheltered against storms by a dense growth of trees, whose midst Noelle eagerly penetrated. The dogs followed, shaking their shaggy coats.

Though small, the island reflected in minute detail the characteristics of the mainland, being all shades of brown and green, flecked with the whitish grey of granite outcrops, the gold of gorse and the purple of heather. Ruined stones suggested an old dwelling place, perhaps the ancient hermitage of one of the many monks with whose history Ireland abounded?

It didn't take long to circuit the island's small circumference and, this achieved, Noelle realised that she was extremely hungry. A pity she hadn't thought to bring a packed lunch with her, but when she had set out, her intentions had been too nebulous for planning ahead. Still, food she must have, and the only way to satisfy her need was to row back across the lough.

It would be prudent to leave now in any case, she

realised as she reached the water's edge. The closely growing trees had concealed the fact that what had been a brisk breeze had become a stiffer force, more to be reckoned with, and the widely spaced clouds were bunching solidly together.

Her strokes were not as vigorous on the return journey, and her sore hands protested at this further assault on their soft skin. To add to her troubles, the wind was increasing, occasional squalls hitting the surface of the lough, making the rowing boat lurch crazily. During one of these onslaughts, Noelle caught a cramp and felt the oar slip from her aching grasp. Making a desperate grab at it, she rocked the boat still further and it capsized.

Noelle was by no means a coward, but even so she could not repress a scream as she felt the surprisingly cold waters engulf her. Her mouth full, initially she sank and rose floundering, sternly admonishing herself not to panic. She had covered more than half the distance between island and shore before the accident occurred, and she was quite capable of swimming the rest.

But the actual rowing had fatigued her more than she knew and she was making slow progress when cramp gripped her left leg. Cramp was still the worst enemy of however brave, however strong a swimmer, and Noelle knew real terror.

The fleeting glimpse of two shaggy heads sturdily breasting the waters side by side gave her her only hope.

'Cleo! Caesar? Here, good dogs!' she cried, and to her amazement, but also to her relief, they responded. She grasped Caesar's collar, and with the bitch in close attendance the strong dog, even with Noelle's added weight, made short work of the remaining distance to the shore.

She dragged herself on to the grassy bank and must have blacked out for a moment or two, for it was the rasping of a large tongue against her cheek which roused her. She sat up, and in a surge of gratitude flung her arms about the shaggy neck.

'Oh, Caesar,' she said aloud, 'I'll never, ever be afraid of you again! Do you know,' she spoke to him as to a human, 'that you've just saved my life?'

A thumping tail answered her, and Cleo too pressed closer for her share of praise.

Thus, dripping wet, a hand on each equally wet collar, Noelle returned to Claddagh, and thus, newly back from England, Fergus saw them coming towards him.

'God in heaven!' He hurried towards her. 'What have you been doing with yourself?'

'I capsized,' she said simply. Reaction was setting in—at least, she told herself, that was what it must be, not just the sight of him—and her legs were shaking uncontrollably.

'What the hell were you doing out in a boat on your own, and in this weather?' he demanded, as he grasped her arm and propelled her towards the house.

'Would you believe—rowing?' she quipped, falsely sweet, hurt that he should be angered rather than concerned. 'Anyway, I wasn't alone.'

'Oh!' At once he was suspicious. 'Byrne was with you, I suppose? You didn't manage to drown him by any chance?' It was half-humorously said, but

Noelle was in no frame of mind for subtleties.

'No, much as I know it would please you. Patrick's quite safe. When I said I wasn't alone, I meant I had the dogs with me.'

By this time they were mounting the main staircase, but Fergus stopped.

'Yes, I knew there was something odd. Just what were they doing with you? You can't stand them.'

'They followed me, and I think Caesar just saved my life. After that—well, I realised just how silly it was to be afraid of them.'

'Wonders will never cease!' Fergus exclaimed. 'Even dogs can be mistaken, a fact I would never have subscribed to.'

'I beg your pardon?'

'I was implying that even dogs can be bad judges of character—but you shouldn't be standing about in that state. Get into a hot bath right away.'

'No, I want to know what you meant by that crack?'

'And I intend to tell you, never fear, but later! Now, are you sure you can manage on your own?'

'Yes,' she retorted, 'and if I can't, I'll call Siobhan.'

'Now what else would I have meant?' was his parting shot.

What indeed? she thought drearily, as she ran the bath. For she was not on those sort of terms with Fergus, and as she luxuriated in the foaming, fragrant water, she imagined just how it would be to have him present, supporting her, perhaps even soaping her body with his lean, powerful fingers. A sensuous shudder ran through her, and before imagination could take her further, she rose, draining the bath, towelling herself vigorously as if to dispel such notions.

Though it would serve no earthly purpose of course, Noelle took great pains with her appearance before going downstairs. It was obvious that Fergus was spoiling for conflict, and she felt in need of every scrap of self-confidence she could muster. As she had guessed, her efforts drew no comment from Fergus, though Miss O'Rourke did exclaim over her dress, one Noelle had not worn before at Claddagh.

'My dear, how very attractive you look. I don't think I've ever seen you in pink before, and such an unusual shade. You should wear that colour more often with your lovely dark colouring. Don't you agree, Fergus?'

His appraising glance was cool and, Noelle thought, hostile, an intuition speedily confirmed by his words.

'Oh, Noelle certainly knows how to dress in the best of taste, and surprisingly expensively too. Did you buy that out of your commission from Cohen?'

Uncomprehendingly, she stared at him. He was referring to Manny, obviously, but what did he mean by that remark about commission? Surely he hadn't found out about Noelle et Cie?'

'Oh, don't give me that wide-eyed wonder! It won't wash. Aunt Bridie,' he turned to Miss O'Rourke, 'take a look at this. I picked it up yesterday, to read on the flight. Just as well I did.'

It was an English newspaper that he had tossed into his great-aunt's lap and Noelle moved to look over her shoulder. The paper was folded open at the arts section and with growing understanding and dismay she read.

'Art Sensation!' the headlines declared. 'Wealthy dress designer, Manny Cohen, declines to comment.' There followed a paragraph of purple prose describing three landscape paintings which had recently appeared for sale at Sotheby's. 'Three works whose existence had been hitherto unsuspected, and identified by experts as the work of . . .' there followed the name of a famous eighteenth-century Irish painter of whom even Noelle had heard—— '. . . whose signature was revealed after professional cleaning had been carried out on the works.'

'No wonder that friend of yours was so anxious to have them,' said Fergus when he saw that Noelle and her aunt had finished reading. 'No wonder he was willing to part with all that money. Just look at the price they fetched! "Wealthy Manny Cohen!" He's even wealthier now, isn't he, and how much did he slip you to keep quiet about the find?'

'Now look here——' Noelle began, then stopped. She had been about to declare that neither she nor Manny had had any idea in the world of the identity or value of their find, but then that didn't tally with Manny's description of himself as an art expert and collector. When she had entered into her benevolent conspiracy with the Cohens she had never expected such an outcome. To both of them, the landscapes had been rather dismal scenes of little aesthetic value, never mind commercial worth. In fact, if it hadn't been for her own facetious suggestion that they be hung in the salon, and for

Rachel's passion for order and cleanliness, the artist's signature and style might never have been discovered.

What on earth, she wondered, had made the Cohens, who knew less about art than she did herself, send the paintings to Sotheby's?

Fergus took her sudden silence as proof of guilt, and with a scornful look he turned on his heel.

'I'll tell Siobhan I won't be in for dinner,' he told Miss O'Rourke. 'Somehow I don't feel inclined to break bread with present company, yourself excluded, Aunt Bridie!'

Since only the three of them were present, the insult was unnecessarily pointed, but Noelle could think of no fitting retort.

'Noelle, you must let me tell him now,' Miss O'Rourke exclaimed after Fergus had left the house. 'You can't let him go on thinking——'

'I can and I'm going to,' Noelle said from between set lips. 'He's known me all these weeks, yet he still believes me capable of dishonesty.' Her voice wavered, then strengthened. 'I forbid you to tell him.'

'But surely he'll have to know some day, and then he'll feel so——'

'Let him,' said Noelle, 'it will do him good to have his arrogant assumptions deflated.'

'But this friend of yours, Mr Cohen. It does rather look as if he's cheated you?'

'Never,' Noelle declared. 'I'd trust Manny with my last penny. The Cohens love making money, but not dishonestly. There'll be a perfectly reasonable explanation.'

There was. And it came next day in the form of a letter, much adorned with exclamation marks, from Rachel. It enclosed a cheque for a very satisfactory amount.

'Dear Noelle,' Rachel's letter read, 'I hope my letter reaches you before the news breaks. So many customers showed interest in your little Irish pictures that we decided to get a professional opinion. Imagine our astonishment when the man from Sotheby's hinted at what they might fetch! They did, and more! I'm enclosing a cheque for the amount over and above what you paid for them. It should help your little project, no?'

It certainly would, Noelle thought. With this money they could clear all of her father's outstanding debts, and the balance left would make a useful foundation on which to rebuild Claddagh's prosperity. The cheque was made payable to Claddagh Estates, a title Fergus and Noelle had decided upon to represent their joint interests. She couldn't show Fergus the letter, of course, its contents revealed too much, but she would take a great pleasure in handing him the cheque, which fortunately the Cohens had had the foresight to draw on their personal account and not that of Noelle et Cie.

Trembling with an anticipation that was half excitement, half fear of his reactions, she tracked him down to the farm office, where he brooded over which of the unpaid bills to settle first.

He hadn't spoken to her since yesterday, and he looked up abruptly as she entered, his eyes asking the question his firmly set lips refused to utter.

'Don't bother sorting through those any more!' Noelle let the cheque flutter on the desk. 'Just pay the lot.' Her triumphant line delivered, she turned away, and she had reached the door again before his voice halted her.

'Where did you get this, and what does it mean?'

'As you can see from the signature,' she said, her voice ringing out with conscious vindication, 'it came from the Cohens, and it means that despite your low opinion of us, my friends and I are not dishonest.' Again she would have left, but this time he prevented her physically, deftly inserting himself between her and the door.

'Then tell me,' he said, brown eyes narrowed, 'just why this "friend" of yours should buy pictures, allegedly for his own collection, sell them at enormous profit, but not, as he was entitled to do— since I was so gullible—keep that profit for himself?'

Elevated chin, sparkling eyes rashly defied him.

'In selling them, Manny was acting for me, not for himself. He isn't a collector, as it happens, and he didn't realise their potential value. He knows nothing about art. He was acting purely as my friend.'

As soon as the words were out she realised that her indignant defence had only clouded the issue still more.

'You're telling me that Cohen is such a *good* friend of yours that he'll pay astronomical sums for pictures he believes to be worthless, not even knowing he could resell them for what he paid, let alone make a profit? What *kind* of friend is he, Noelle?'

Put that way it sounded suspiciously illogical, hinting at a relationship of the kind she had already denied. She was tempted then to tell Fergus the whole truth, but he went on.

'Thank God you did refuse to marry me, and thank God those pictures did sell at a profit.' He paused, then: 'At least Cohen was astute enough to deduct *your* "price".'

For a moment she stood staring at him, not fully taking in his implication, then, as it slowly dawned on her, her face went, not red, but sickly pale with shock, her tongue cleaving drily to the roof of her mouth. She was mistress enough of herself not to break down, not to burst into frenzied denials. Instead she shot him a look of utter loathing and turned on her heel, the door closing deliberately soundlessly behind her.

For the rest of that day and the whole of the next, Noelle remained in the lethargy of shock. In part she supposed she could not blame Fergus for his misunderstanding of the situation, since to a certain extent it was due to her own secretiveness. But the fact that he could so immediately jump to the conclusion that he had was what hurt her badly.

This belief of his was a profanation of all her ideals. She knew she had the capacity for giving herself utterly and without reserve to the right man if he ever appeared to claim her, but that Fergus should think that she would do so for any man for monetary gain was the ultimate insult.

And besides, would Fergus himself be any better, if he were to marry Suzanne for financial reasons? Unless, of course, he was also in love with the other girl.

She had cause again to wonder about their exact relationship when Suzanne called. Returning from a walk with the dogs, Noelle found Miss O'Rourke entertaining the other girl, who seemed unperturbed to find that Fergus was out and quite prepared to await his return. She sat with Noelle and Miss O'Rourke, her conversation full of the recent week in England, and London in particular.

'How I'd love to live in England!' she enthused. 'There was so much to see. I could have spent months in London alone. We went to the parks and the art galleries, the Tower, stood outside Buckingham Palace, waiting to see if the Queen would come out.'

Fergus must have a lot more patience than she gave him credit for, Noelle mused, if he was prepared to traipse all around London visiting places that surely must be already familiar to him. Still, it was wonderful what love could achieve, she mused wryly, otherwise why was she herself remaining in Ireland to be hurt over and over again?

'And was Fergus able to find time, amidst all this sightseeing, to attend to the sale of his farm?'

Did Suzanne sense the jealousy behind her remark? Certainly she looked at Noelle very oddly before replying.

'It didn't interfere with his business at all.'

'Did your parents enjoy the trip?' Miss O'Rourke

put in hastily as though she too sensed a slight atmosphere.

'I believe so. I hardly saw anything of them. They had their own plans.'

So Suzanne and Fergus had been alone for most of the time!

'Did you see Uncle John while you were in London?' Noelle knew that John Madox-Browne, on leaving Ireland, had issued the traditional invitation to 'drop in and see me if you're ever in my part of the world'.

'Oh yes, we did. He's very nice, isn't he?' Suzanne said almost vaguely, thus disposing of that conversational gambit. 'I'll tell you who else we saw. Patrick was in London, did you know?'

'I knew he was visiting relations,' said Noelle, 'but I didn't know where.'

Suzanne finally rose to leave.

'Don't forget to tell Fergus I was here, and,' she spoke particularly to Miss O'Rourke, 'you'll not forget to bring up the subject I mentioned . . .?'

Miss O'Rourke nodded, and Noelle felt the flare of jealousy within her at the knowledge that Suzanne and Miss O'Rourke, and presumably Fergus, had secrets she did not share.

Noelle knew she wouldn't tell him about Suzanne's visit because they weren't speaking again, but the task could safely be left to her great-aunt, who now made it clear she had sensed Noelle's animosity.

'Tell me, Noelle, do you think Suzanne has her eye on Fergus?'

'Yes,' Noelle said shortly.

'And don't you mind?' Her tone indicated her belief that Noelle must do so.

Noelle looked at Bridie O'Rourke, about to strenuously deny the fact, then:

'Yes,' she said bleakly, 'I mind, very much.'

'Fergus might be very interested to know that,' Miss O'Rourke suggested tentatively.

'Oh yes, I daresay!' Noelle retorted. 'That *would* be something for him to gloat over, the fact that I've fallen hopelessly in love with him, a man who distrusts and despises me!'

'That need not be so,' Miss O'Rourke pointed out. 'You have too much pride, Noelle. A little straight talking from you would soon clear up all the misunderstandings. And then you might find out that he feels very differently about you.'

'There's been no misunderstanding so far as I'm concerned. Fergus made his hostility clear right from the beginning. It was only because of his attitude that I had to do good for Claddagh by devious means. And I know how he feels about me. He's made that clear too.'

Miss O'Rourke appeared unconvinced.

'You know, my dear, Fergus was a very mischievous boy. He had a delightfully odd sense of humour. I can't believe that the man has become so very much different from the boy. Don't you think that a lot of the time he may have been teasing you?'

Noelle considered the possibilities of her great-aunt's suggestion, which, to be honest, had occurred to her once or twice, but she shook her head.

'Even if he was in the beginning, he isn't now. He really believed the accusations he made against

Manny and me.'

'Couldn't that be jealousy?' Miss O'Rourke still sounded hopeful.

'No, not when he's got Suzanne.'

'Oh, but——'

'. . . and the prospect of all her father's money some day,' Noelle went on as if her aunt hadn't spoken. 'If he's jealous of anything at all, it's of my half share in Claddagh; he's afraid I'll marry Patrick and involve *him* in Claddagh affairs.'

'But you wouldn't? Not just to spite Fergus, I mean?' Miss O'Rourke asked anxiously.

'No,' Noelle sighed, 'I wouldn't. Marriage is far too important to be treated so lightly. But,' warningly, 'Fergus doesn't have to know that. And there's something else I don't intend to do either, and that's meekly sell out to him and be driven away. Claddagh is as much my home now as his.'

'Oh dear, oh dear!' Miss O'Rourke's worried frown was in evidence again. 'I do wish things could have resolved themselves without my interference!'

'Your interference?' Immediately Noelle was suspicious. 'What do you mean? Aunt Bridie, don't you dare say a word to Fergus about my feelings for him, or about anything else! Remember, you promised!'

'And I'll keep *that* promise,' Bridie O'Rourke told her, but her next words did not relieve Noelle's uneasiness, 'but there are certain steps I'm afraid I shall just have to take.' And further than that she refused to be drawn.

'Suzanne was here this afternoon,' Miss O'Rourke

said conversationally to her great-nephew as the three of them sat down to their evening meal. It was an occasion which Noelle had dreaded, the conversation stilted, with Miss O'Rourke the only one willing to communicate with both sides. 'She had such a lot to tell us. She certainly seems to have enjoyed her visit to England.'

'Yes.' Fergus sounded surprisingly cheerful, quite unlike the black mood he had been in for the previous forty-eight hours. 'She's easy to please and good company.'

'That sounds as though you're rather fond of her?'

Did her aunt have to probe this particular wound? Noelle brooded.

'Oh, I am,' Fergus returned, 'always have been, you know that. It's splendid having her as a neighbour, instead of our once or twice a year encounters.'

'I've always been very surprised,' Miss O'Rourke said casually, 'that she never married. I've always thought she'd make an excellent wife, efficient as well as attractive.'

If this was her great-aunt's notion of interference, Noelle wished she would stop it. She had no wish to hear the other girl's praises sung by Fergus. Its only effect could be to confirm what she most dreaded to hear.

'Her social life has been rather limited,' Fergus observed, 'but things have improved of late.'

Since *his* arrival at Claddagh, of course, Noelle thought, aware of her heart's panicky flutterings in her throat. For a moment it seemed that same heart had completely ceased operation when he added,

'But now I think there may soon be an announcement.'

Miss O'Rourke put her head on one side in an oddly bird-like gesture that for an instant made her look like the mischievous girl she must once have been.

'To anyone we know?' she enquired with a curious little smile.

Fergus's only reply was an upward curve of his mouth, an irritating triumph of secretive insinuation, but his brown eyes were fixed upon Noelle's face.

During this conversation she had tried valiantly to continue eating, but her brave efforts were to prove disastrous. Her growing conviction that Fergus was withholding an announcement which concerned him as well as Suzanne, proved too much for her already rebellious nerves. She felt her stomach heave, and with an anguished gasp she left the table and fled before she could disgrace herself.

In the bathroom she was violently sick with an inner retching that tore her through and through, each spasm accompanied by a hiccuping sob. As she ran the cold tap to lave her face and rinse her mouth, she did not hear the rapid footsteps and as she turned to leave, intending to go to her room, she encountered Fergus in the doorway.

His expression, which usually varied between mockery and suspicion, seemed to hold only concern.

'Something disagreed with you?' he asked, but as she nodded, glad of this ready-made excuse, he went on, 'Nothing *I* said, I hope?'

'Of course not!' Though still shaking she had regained a little of her normal aplomb. 'How could it be?'

'It seemed to follow very quickly upon the subject of Suzanne. I wondered if you had any reason for disliking her?'

'None whatsoever.' It was said a little stiffly, but it was true. She did like Suzanne, for herself, if not as a prospective cousin-in-law.

'Then you would welcome her, quite happily, as a member of your family?'

Noelle found she had no answer to this, or at least not one she could safely utter. She could only stare at Fergus, her blue eyes wide with fear as she willed him not to say the words she dreaded hearing. She must have turned unusually pale, for Fergus took a quick step nearer, his hand grasping her arm.

'What is it? Are you ill? Still feeling sick?'

She could only shake her head.

'Come on now, Noelle,' he said, almost coaxing-ly, 'what's upset you, then?' His voice grew harder, 'It must be something to do with Suzanne. She was our only topic of conversation.' His eyes narrowed as still she made no reply. 'Do you know more about it than I . . .'

'No,' she denied, but he swept on.

'You do. You know and don't like the idea? I thought I'd come to know you pretty well these last few weeks, and whatever other faults you may have I would never have expected such pettiness, such jealousy of someone else's happiness. What can it possibly matter to you? How can it affect you? Unless . . .?'

It was all moving too fast for Noelle. What did he suspect, know? She couldn't follow the drift of his impassioned speech. She felt light-headed and not a little faint.

'Please let me go. I think I need to lie down for a while.'

'It's affected you that badly?' But he didn't release her. 'Just what were you expecting, I wonder? But no ... it'd be a long wait, scarcely worthwhile ...' He was still talking in riddles as far as she was concerned, and he continued to study her drawn face, the tremulous quivering of her mouth. 'What you need, my girl, is something more important to concentrate on, an interest of your own.' Having said which, he pulled her, unresisting, for she was not expecting it, into his embrace.

His kiss was sensuous, searching, his thighs steely hard, unyielding against hers, and the movements of his hands arousing, wrecking any attempt she might make to think clearly about his inconsistent behaviour.

The pressure of his body grew in intensity, as he explored the swell of her breasts, and Noelle found herself trembling violently beneath his determined onslaught. His every action was passionate, possessive, yet punishing too, as his teeth worried her lower lip. She became aware as never before of his body, its contours, its needs, telling her that he wanted her in spite of ... in spite of Suzanne! Noelle's head cleared with horrible suddenness at the realisation of what he was doing to her, of how unscrupulously he was behaving. But just as she was about to fight for her freedom, he released her.

'And what,' he said, and his voice was shaken, husky, 'have you to say to that?'

'Just this,' she wrenched free of him, 'that you're despicable!'

'In what way, for God's sake?' Clearly it wasn't the answer he had expected. He sounded surprised, affronted, the hypocrite!

'Your behaviour, that's what. Making me ... when you ... People about to be married don't behave in that way with somebody else, not in my book anyhow.'

'People about to be married?' He repeated her words. 'I see!' It was said on an indrawn hiss of breath. Then, more strongly, 'Yes, I see. Well, at least we now know exactly where we stand.' He turned away, then back again to ask in biting tones, 'And are we to assume that *you'll* still go on living here, afterwards?'

Noelle felt as if her pain must be visible, that it must surely be severing her in two before his eyes, but she forced herself to answer defiantly.

'Why? Did you think you'd be rid of me that way? No chance!'

'I see,' he said again. 'In that case I may have to rethink my own plans. Maybe I'd better be the one to leave.'

And she didn't have to wonder long to know where he'd go, Noelle thought miserably. The Faheys would as gladly welcome their son-in-law into their home as into their family, and where would that leave her? With Claddagh, a prize that had lost all its value.

CHAPTER EIGHT

'THEN you'll sell me your half of Claddagh?' Noelle asked, forgetting that as far as Fergus knew she was no better off than he. But he showed no surprise.

'No. I'm afraid you'll still have to account to me for my share of the property. You're not getting everything your way, my girl.' She might have known Fergus was not a man to give up so easily.

Now, more than ever before, Noelle avoided Fergus. But distancing herself from him didn't make her any happier. It only gave her more time to reflect on what had passed between them, to analyse the motive for his bitter words, to try and construe their meaning. Obviously, he had guessed how unacceptable to her would be his proposed marriage to Suzanne, and he had been bitterly angry with her because of it. But had he also guessed at her reason? She hoped not. For her pride's sake she would rather he attributed it to a dog-in-the-manger attitude where Claddagh Hall was concerned than that he should guess how much she herself loved him.

If only she could root out that love! But it was impossible, even though she listed for herself over and over again the reasons why she should hate Fergus, not the least the fact that he should kiss and caress her in such an intimate fashion, when he knew she was aware of his attachment to Suzanne.

It shamed her every time she remembered how, for a few seconds, she had responded, with all the pent-up longing of her hungry heart and body. She could only hope that Fergus was not too perceptive of the differences between male and female attitudes to love and sex.

Initially his kiss had been intended as a form of punishment, she was sure of that, but then the primitive male in him had become aroused, something Noelle knew had only happened to her because she loved, not from sheer physical attraction.

Miss O'Rourke had shown great concern over Noelle's sudden indisposition, and when they were alone she scolded her great-niece.

'You've been overdoing things, my dear—the decorating, your trip to London, all that on top of nursing me through my illness. Fergus was most concerned.'

'He has a strange way of showing it!'

'He was being unnecessarily mysterious about Suzanne, surely?' Miss O'Rourke went on, watching Noelle keenly. 'She has discussed her plans with me and she asked me to tell you——'

'Why?' Noelle said bitterly. 'It's nothing to do with me.'

'It will affect you, in a way——'

'Because he plans to marry her, you mean? I'm sure I couldn't care less,' she lied.

'Oh, but——' Miss O'Rourke began, when once again she was interrupted.

'Did I hear my name being mentioned?' Fergus stood in the doorway of Miss O'Rourke's sitting room, his tall, lithe figure immaculately dressed for riding. 'On Noelle's lips I can be certain no compliment was intended.'

How long had he been listening, Noelle wondered with a tremor of alarm, and had he learned anything from their conversation?

'Only conceited people are always imagining themselves the target for discussion,' she said, her tone intentionally rude to hide her confusion.

Miss O'Rourke rushed into the breach.

'In actual fact we were just discussing Suzanne, wondering when the wedding would be. I promised I'd tell Noelle——'

'Yes, I suppose Noelle in particular would be concerned about that!' Fergus's tone was ironic and Noelle flushed, looking at Bridie O'Rourke. Surely her great-aunt hadn't broken her promise?

'It's a matter of complete indifference to me,' she said.

'Oh? But surely you'll have the grace to wish the girl happiness?' probed Fergus, his manner decidedly provoking, and Noelle was certain that even if her aunt were not the culprit, Fergus had his suspicions as to the state of her feelings for him, a suspicion that must immediately be quelled.

'Fergus!' Miss O'Rourke tried again. 'I do think you might let me . . .'

'I'll wish her happiness, certainly,' Noelle said coolly, 'but I doubt if she'll achieve it, in view of the husband she's chosen.'

If she had expected her words to achieve an

effect, she was not disappointed, but instead of the torrent of angry words she had expected, she was surprised to receive Fergus's look of utter contempt.

'And I suppose you'll enjoy telling her that, too?' he said tautly.

Though appalled by her own words, by the enormity of the breach she was putting between them, Noelle found she was past caring. It didn't matter what she did or said now. Fergus was lost to her, had never been hers in any case, and she could better salvage her pride if he thought that meant nothing.

'If she were to ask my advice, I should certainly feel it was my duty to say so.'

Noelle's shaking legs continued to hold her until Fergus turned on his heel and his riding boots could be heard clattering down the stairs. Then she sank into a chair, covering her face with her hands. Through her misery, she heard the shuffle of Miss O'Rourke's slippered feet on the carpet, and then her great-aunt's hand rested on her shoulder.

'There, there, my dear. Oh, how foolish young people are, so hasty-tongued! If only Fergus hadn't walked in when he did, before I'd had time to break the news to you gently. You're so quick to anger with each other. You see, I didn't realise you already knew about Suzanne, and I must admit I didn't think you'd take it so hard. You have such a generous nature as a rule.'

'I shouldn't have said what I did,' Noelle admitted. 'I like the girl, heaven help me, and I wouldn't hurt her for the world. I wouldn't really tell her what I think, but Fergus made me so angry. But,' reproachfully, 'I thought you at least would understand how it hurts to know Fergus is going to marry Suzanne, when I——'

'Then you know nothing!' Miss O'Rourke exclaimed. She sounded unusually stern and Noelle was surprised into silence, an effect Bridie had probably intended. 'Suzanne Fahey isn't going to marry *Fergus*.'

'Not . . .?'

'Certainly not! If she marries anyone, and I gather he hasn't actually asked her in so many words, but that he will after a suitable period, it will be John Madox-Browne.'

'Uncle John?' Noelle echoed disbelievingly. 'But they hardly know each other!'

'Suzanne took a great fancy to him when he came here to visit and when she was in London they met again. It seems the attraction was mutual. But out of respect for your mother and consideration for you nothing definite was decided on. Suzanne confided in me, and I was supposed to find out your feelings on the subject.'

'My feelings!' Noelle was radiant with the uprush of joy that Fergus was not, after all, to be married. 'I'd be so happy for John if he were to marry again. It's what I'd hoped for, though I didn't think it would be so soon. He loved my mother very much.' Then the full implications of the situation began to dawn on her and she cast her mind back over her hasty exchange of words with Fergus. 'Heavens! Fergus must think I wanted to put Suzanne off Uncle John,' she realised.

'I'm afraid so, and the two of you were arguing so fiercely I couldn't make myself heard to tell him you had no idea.'

'No wonder he was so disgusted with me!'

'You two young things,' Miss O'Rourke sighed, 'are typical O'Rourkes, rash, impulsive. Speak first, understand too late. Don't you think it's time you put the record straight between you, about a lot of things?'

'But I can't,' Noelle declared. 'Don't you see? If I explain that I didn't know about John and Suzanne, he'll wonder what on earth all the fuss was about, and knowing Fergus it won't take long for him to work it out. It would be so humiliating.'

'Humiliating! Pah!' For the first time since Noelle had known her great-aunt, Bridie displayed evidence that she too was very much one of the fiery O'Rourkes. 'It's time you got your priorities right. Young people these days make too much of their pride. All that's required of you is a simple apology. So what if Fergus guesses that you love him . . . and you never know where that might lead! It's nothing to be ashamed of, is it?'

'No,' Noelle had to admit, 'but . . .'

'But nothing! Do it, girl, apologise, explain, unless you want to end up a withered, lonely old woman like me.'

Noelle's discernment was swift.

'You mean there was an occasion when you should have apologised?'

Miss O'Rourke held herself erect.

'There was, and I'm not proud of it. So you learn from my experience. It's my guess you'll be surprised at Fergus's reaction. Do it now, before the wounds you've dealt each other fester still more. A man has his pride too.'

'I can't,' said Noelle with craven relief at the reprieve. 'Fergus is out and I don't know where.'

'But I do. He's hacking a gelding across to the Faheys, one that Terence Fahey is buying for his riding school. If you take the car you can be there almost as soon. Talk to Suzanne too, kill two birds with one stone.'

Noelle wasn't sure that she ought to be driving, she felt so nervous about confronting Fergus. How could she get him to listen to her in the first place? And when she had explained, apologised, what then?

The first person she saw as she drove on to the forecourt of the Fahey's house was Suzanne. She too was dressed for riding, and seeing how the clothes became her, Noelle found herself regretting that she had never learnt to ride a horse.

'Noelle?' Suzanne's greeting was friendly, yet a little apprehensive. 'Has Miss O'Rourke told you? Do you mind very much?'

In the face of these eager questions, Noelle was only too glad to postpone her forthcoming ordeal, and she didn't enquire for Fergus.

'Yes, Aunt Bridie told me and I'm delighted, honestly. I hope you and John will be very happy. He's the kindest of men.'

'Oh!' Suzanne's tense shoulders sagged on a breath of relief. 'And I was so afraid you might resent my loving John because of your mother. And then Fergus said you might well expect to be John's heir some day, and I do so hope . . ., the other girl flushed becomingly, '. . . that I'm not too old to give him children of his own.'

The reason for some of Fergus's angry remarks was becoming very clear.

'I've never expected a penny from John,' Noelle said firmly, 'or needed it.' She hesitated, wondering whether to confide in Suzanne about Noelle et Cie. But the moment was lost in the ring of metal-shod hooves on cobbles as Fergus rode across the courtyard.

His keen eyes had taken in the confidential manner between the two girls, and his face hardened as he looked at Noelle.

'Sorry to interrupt your girlish gossip. Could you take charge of this old fellow for me, Suzanne? I want to get back.' He dismounted. 'I see Noelle has very considerately provided my transport home.'

'I didn't come here for that,' Noelle began, automatically on the defensive.

'Oh, I'm sure you didn't!' was the biting reply. 'But since you are here . . . and on the way back you can tell me exactly why you did come and how far you've achieved your purpose.'

Suzanne was staring from one to the other in mild astonishment.

'Don't mind us, Sue,' Fergus told her. 'You know the O'Rourkes, just a family quarrel.' Peremptorily he motioned Noelle towards the passenger seat and took the wheel himself.

Outside the boundary of the Fahey property, Fergus swung the car left instead of right towards

Claddagh Hall.

'I thought you wanted to get home,' said Noelle, unable to stand the grim silence any longer.

'No. I think it's best we have this discussion on neutral territory,' he returned. 'Our resolution not to argue in front of Aunt Bridie has wavered again of late and I have a feeling this is going to prove even more acrimonious than usual.'

'If you'd just let me explain first,' Noelle began.

'Not yet,' he said curtly. 'When I'm driving I like to give it my full attention. You'll have your say soon enough, and I shall certainly have mine!'

They were driving north, Lough Corrib always within sight, and at its northernmost point, where an isthmus divided it from Lough Mask, Fergus stopped. He came round the car and indicated that Noelle too should get out.

She had no objection. The confines of the car were altogether too close to endure the aura of his anger that still seemed to engulf them both.

'The two lakes are connected here by an underground river,' Fergus commented as they walked, and Noelle stopped short, turning on him.

'You didn't bring me here for a geography lesson. Either get to the point or let me say what I have to.'

'All right.' His tone was grim as he grasped her elbow and propelled her on towards the water's edge. 'I want to know exactly what you said to Suzanne about your stepfather and just how far your mischief succeeded.'

Incensed, Noelle tried to snatch her arm from his grasp.

'That just goes to show you should have listened

to me first. I told Suzanne I was very happy to hear about her and John, that I'd always hoped he would marry again some day.'

If she hadn't been so angry, so unhappy, she might have found amusement at having so completely undermined the grounds for his complaint against her.

'You did! Then what the hell was all the fuss about earlier?' He lowered himself to the springy turf, pulling her down with him, keeping hold of her arm as she glared at him.

'That was you, jumping to conclusions as usual.'

'Which is a fault you never display, of course.' He had recovered his aplomb and his tone was sarcastic as he made the telling remark.

'I may do,' she said defensively, 'but not as often as you. You assumed that I knew about Suzanne and John, whereas I knew nothing of the sort. Aunt Bridie has only just told me.'

'Then you thought . . .' With his free hand, Fergus began to finger his beard, a reflective habit he sometimes had, and Noelle knew this was her last opportunity to save face, if she wanted to.

'I thought the poor girl was going to be mad enough to marry you, in which case I should certainly have advised her against it.' The words were defiant, but somehow her voice didn't carry conviction and Fergus's mouth twisted into a wry smile.

'You would, would you?' His grasp of her arm tightened. 'And what makes you think it would be so bad?'

'Personal observation and experience!' she flung at him.

'Observation I'll grant you,' he said drily. 'Though I'm not sure I personally would rely too much on your powers in that direction. But experience?' There was a dangerous glint in the brown eyes. 'I fail to see how you can claim that?'

'I meant,' she said hastily, 'experience of your abominable insults, your insinuations. Half the time I don't know whether you're serious, or if you're just being provoking.'

'And there you have it in a nutshell,' he said with irritating satisfaction. 'You don't know me at all, and you've never given me a chance to get to know you. Why, I wonder?'

As he spoke, he had edged closer to her, his eyes holding hers in such thrall that she felt certain he could see into her soul, read her innermost thoughts, and she was afraid of what she might reveal.

In that moment of exquisite tension, she found herself desperately searching her memory for some accusation worth hurling at him. But taken separately, diluted already by her love for him, every annoying incident had shrunk to a mere pinprick of an irritation.

But Fergus didn't intend to wait long for the answer to his question. A hand under her chin forced her to go on meeting his gaze.

'You can't answer me. Shall I tell you why? Sheer perverseness, Noelle. You see, I had you weighed up the moment we met. Your reactions were wholly predictable. You not only look like your father, you have his volatile temperament. You rose to every bait I threw out.'

'Then that makes you more to blame than me, if you deliberately . . . Oh, I detest you!'

'No, you don't,' he confounded her by saying. 'However unwillingly, Noelle, you find me attractive to you. O.K., so my tactics were all wrong. I admit there's a better way of dealing with argumentative females, of showing them how wrong they can be.' He grasped her by the shoulders and there was a sudden stillness between them, a waiting that played havoc with her nerves. She was acutely aware of impending danger, suddenly recklessly unwilling to evade it. She didn't want to argue with Fergus any more, had only kept it going this long from sheer nervousness.

'Have you ever belonged to that fellow Cohen?' he asked harshly.

The question was totally unexpected. Noelle shook her head, unable to speak, her lips were so dry. Nervously she edged the tip of her tongue over them, but not discreetly enough, for she saw his eyes darken almost to black in their intensity.

'And has Byrne ever made love to you?'

Noelle felt the sudden elation of power. The answers to his questions mattered to Fergus, she realised, really mattered. She allowed her eyelids to flicker down, deliberately demure.

'He has kissed me once or twice,' she admitted.

'Don't play games, Noelle.' He was stern now. 'You know what I mean!'

Her eyes opened wide, their blue depths now as earnest as his own.

'No one has ever done more than that,' she told

him throatily, and felt her whole body throb with charged suspense.

'Why is that, Noelle?' The words hung between them, the answer marking a vital point in their relationship.

'I've never met anyone who meant that much to me.' Somehow she was still able to meet his gaze.

'Until now?' Silence. 'Noelle?' Her name on his lips was a caressing sound. 'I believe I could mean that much to you.' Still silence. 'Noelle?'

'I . . . I don't know. I told you, I don't know how *you* feel. You always seemed to dislike me. When I told you to stop proposing to me, you were relieved, admit it!'

Temporarily he ignored the statement.

'Do you dislike me, then?'

'I . . . no, I don't dislike you.' Her heart was pounding violently beneath her ribs.

'You told me to stop proposing a marriage of convenience,' he reminded her, 'and I agreed because the next time I ask you it's going to be a serious proposition. What kind of answer am I likely to get?' and as she shook her head, not in negation but in helpless wonder, he smiled enigmatically.

He did not press her any further, but moved without haste, pushing against the shoulders he still held, until she lay prone, unprotesting, waiting, as he knelt above her. Slowly his eyes explored her, missing no detail, the wide, wondering eyes, tremulous mouth, the shallow, nervous rise and fall of her breasts.

Strong, warm fingers encircled her ankle, his free

hand removing her shoe. He raised her foot to his
mouth, his lips brushing against the sensitive
instep, while his eyes watched her face closely,
studying her reactions. His touch was electrifying.
But still uncertain of his motives, she wasn't going
to accord him such an easy victory. Expressionlessly
she watched him as once more he bent his head and
let his mouth ascend, brushing over the gentle swell
of her bare calf, his fingers moving to grip her knee,
so far and tantalisingly no further.

Large hands moved then to span her waist, as if
measuring it, moved down, smoothing the fine
fabric of her dress over her hips. Noelle caught her
bottom lip in her teeth, willing herself not to
tremble. He was so sure of himself, so certain that
she would succumb, but of his own feelings he had
revealed nothing.

His hands moved upward again, to the pointed
fullness of her small breasts, causing them to swell
and ache beneath the pressure of his lean fingers,
and though it took all her resolution, still she made
no sound, no movement.

He moved to lie beside her, turning her,
gathering her up to him, hard against his body,
while one long leg held her captive, yet still he made
no move to kiss her, though his eyes forbade hers to
lose their concentration upon his face.

'Touch me, Noelle,' he commanded unsteadily. 'I
want you to touch me.'

Totally ensnared by now in the hypnotic web he
had woven about her, she did as he asked. First the
luxuriance of his hair which her hands had often
yearned to caress, then down over the coarser hair

of cheeks and jaw, its roughness a sensuous pricking against her soft palms. She drew a finger over the firmly moulded lips, mutely begging for their kiss, but still he denied her.

Now it was the muscled contours of his chest that knew her tentative voyage of discovery, her hands sliding inside his shirt, feeling the moist warmth of his skin, the softness of body hair.

'Why did you tell me you were going to marry Byrne!' he asked unexpectedly, and she jerked in surprised rejection.

'But I didn't.'

'You said, and I quote, people who were going to be married didn't behave like this.' He demonstrated, a skilful move of his thighs exerting pressure against her, at last bringing the shuddering reaction he sought.

'I . . . I was talking about you, you and Suzanne. I thought . . . ahh!' Her voice trembled away into a sigh as his hands moved with gentle insistence.

'You've never even considered marrying Byrne?' he probed.

'Never!' she insisted. 'Oh, Fergus!' A rash wantonness overtook her and she strained closer to him, placing her mouth on his, urgently seeking, and as if she had set a torchlight to dry tinder she felt his own desire flame as he returned, deepened the kiss she had instigated, his tongue warm and gently probing, lingering with a marvellous intensity, inducing a sensuous surge of feeling within her, the obsessive need to know his entire body. But as she shifted against him in restless excitement, he held her away a little, scanning her warm flushed cheeks, the languorous, passion-induced droop of eyes and mouth.

'My little Noelle!' he said tenderly. 'But no, my love, this is no place to make our final truce. Come home.' His voice thickened. 'Come home to Claddagh and we'll make love under our own roof.'

Half reluctantly she allowed him to pull her to her feet. He held her to his side, their steps matching as they walked slowly back to the car. For a moment in its greater privacy, he held her in a close, passionate embrace, then, as if his urgency could no longer be delayed, he started the car.

He drove fast but skilfully, and Noelle beside him leaned back in her seat, content to study lovingly the profile turned towards her, to dream, to imagine, to anticipate. Silently she blessed Bridie O'Rourke for insisting that she seek Fergus out.

In her euphoric state, it didn't even occur to her that there were still explanations left unmade.

A strange car stood outside the Hall.

'What a time to have visitors!' Fergus groaned, Noelle's hand held tightly in his. 'Let's hope it's just someone for Aunt Bridie and we can sneak past without getting caught.'

His hopes were dashed as the elderly manservant intercepted them in the hallway.

'Miss O'Rourke asked me to look out for you, Mr Fergus. You and Miss Noelle are wanted in the dining room.'

Bridie O'Rourke sat at the long refectory table, her companion's face a familiar one, that of Mr Kelly the family solicitor. Both looked grave and

Miss O'Rourke decidedly nervous. She spoke first.

'Fergus, Noelle, my dears, I have a confession to make. I asked Mr Kelly to come and see me, because it's time my little deception was set right.'

'Little deception!' the solicitor sniffed. 'Fraud, I call it, ma'am, fraud.'

'Here now, hold on,' Fergus intervened, 'just what are you accusing my aunt of?'

'It's true, Fergus,' said Bridie O'Rourke. 'But I always meant to reveal the truth eventually, by which time I hoped you and Noelle . . . But I dared not leave it any longer. My last illness, you see, it frightened me and I thought, suppose I were to be ill again and die before I could put things right.'

'Perhaps I might explain,' Mr Kelly said as Miss O'Rourke showed signs of incoherence.

Put succinctly in Mr Kelly's dry legal terminology, it transpired that the will he had read to them on Fergus's arrival at Claddagh had not been the last one made by Noel O'Rourke.

'His Lordship made that will some years ago, when you, Miss Madox-Browne, were in your teens. When His Lordship heard of Mrs Madox-Browne's death, he wrote to her husband asking to see his daughter. But there was no reply and it seems, unknown to me,' he added severely, 'he drew up a new will, witnessed by two of the servants here, leaving the entire property to Mr Carrick only. Miss O'Rourke knew of this new will and deliberately concealed its existence.'

For a moment the two people most affected sat in stunned silence. Noelle was the first to recover. It wasn't as if she would really be losing Claddagh.

'But that's marvellous!'

'Is it?'

She turned to look at Fergus, found his face contorted in a mixture of anger and anguish.

'Of course it is,' she told him. 'After all, it doesn't matter now which of us it belongs to, because——'

Miss O'Rourke gave a little crow of excitement.

'Do you mean to say you two have actually come to an agreement?'

'No!' Fergus answered before Noelle could speak. 'Nothing of the sort!' He turned on his aunt, the first time Noelle had ever seen him angry with the elderly woman. 'Whatever possessed you to do what you did?'

'It . . . it was when I first met dear Noelle. I loved her at once,' Miss O'Rourke faltered. 'Both of you were unmarried and the idea came to me that if you were thrown together, as Noel originally intended, two such nice people . . . and it would have been so suitable! When the time came for Mr Kelly to read the first will, I was a little afraid of what I'd done.' Noelle remembered Miss O'Rourke's strangely apprehensive manner. 'But I thought I could always put things right, if they didn't turn out the way I planned.'

'And did it never occur to you the disappointment it would cause Noelle, when you did reveal the truth?' Fergus asked savagely.

'No, I'm afraid not, I was so certain, you see, that . . .'

Fergus turned to the solicitor.

'I suppose there's no doubt that this later will is valid?'

'Quite legal and correct, sir.'

'Damn it all to hell!' exploded Fergus, then to his aunt. 'I wish, Aunt Bridie, having once meddled, you'd let well alone. Excuse me,' he made for the door, 'but I have to think this out—alone,' he added warningly, as Noelle made a movement towards him.

CHAPTER NINE

There was a second or two of astonished silence following Fergus's departure, then Mr Kelly cleared his throat and shuffled his papers together.

'I'll be away, then,' he said and, abandoning for a moment his purely professional manner, 'Blessed if I ever saw a man react so strangely to good news!'

Miss O'Rourke seemed disposed to follow up on this topic after the solicitor had left, but Noelle felt that, like Fergus, she needed to be alone to consider this unexpected development.

As was her usual habit when troubled, she set out to walk to the lough side. Exercise, she found, stimulated the thinking process.

Like Mr Kelly, she found it difficult to understand Fergus's anger. It would have been perfectly logical for *her* to react in that way, but she had seen no need, since Fergus had revealed his feelings for her. A marriage between them would effectively solve the problem of ownership. But now he seemed to be denying any such intention on his part.

Then a thought came to her, so dreadful in its implications that she stopped short, the nausea of fear and distaste welling within her. Fergus didn't need to marry her now that Claddagh was exclusively his. His lovemaking must have been a ploy to prevent her marrying elsewhere, bringing in an outsider to further complicate ownership of the property. How relieved he must now be that he had only hinted at a forthcoming proposal, that he was still uncommitted. But, she puzzled, that still didn't explain his outburst of anger.

As she walked, the sight of strenuous activity in and around Patrick's cottage brought a much needed diversion from her troubled musings, and the sight of Patrick himself overseeing the comings and goings of several men aroused her curiosity.

'It looks as though you're moving house?'

'So I am,' he returned.

'But why?'

'Several reasons, all of which add up to the conclusion that it's time I stopped loafing through life.'

Noelle was intrigued, and her expression prompted him to continue.

'There's nothing here for me. Once I thought there might have been.'

'Claddagh?'

'That, and then there was you. Though I admit,' he added, but with no apparent shame, 'that Claddagh was the main attraction.'

'As I suspected,' she told him, but without malice.

'And it obviously makes more sense anyway, for you to marry Fergus Carrick.'

'You said there were other reasons for your move,' she said hurriedly.

Patrick, it seemed, was in love, genuinely this time. While visiting his relations in England, he had met their neighbour's son and through him, the daughter.

'But she won't have anything to do with me at all,' he told Noelle, 'unless I promise to make something of myself.'

Noelle's eyebrows rose incredulously.

'Does she know you're already a rich man?'

'She maintains that inherited wealth doesn't count. "I don't want an idle dilettante for a husband," says she.'

'So you've to earn your living?' Despite her own troubles, Noelle could not repress a smile at the thought of the lotus-eating Patrick actually working. 'When do you go?'

'The day after tomorrow. I've some local business to attend to first.'

'But all your furniture's gone.'

'I'm taking a room in Galway for a couple of nights. Perhaps you'll have a farewell meal with me before I leave?'

'Of course. I would have invited you to stay at the Hall, despite Fergus, but since I've no say in things now . . .'

'You haven't?' It was Patrick's turn to be curious, and suddenly Noelle felt she must confide in someone, someone who now had no vested interest in Claddagh and its ownership.

Briefly she explained the discovery of the new will, omitting only Miss O'Rourke's part in concealing its existence. Patrick gave a low whistle of incredulity.

'So now 'tis all legally his, he's dropped you like a hot brick?'

'It looks that way!' Noelle admitted. 'And it means I'll have to change all my plans. It's a good thing I haven't had time to go into Dublin to see about shop premises.' Then she remembered that Patrick knew nothing about her professional life. He was impressed when she explained.

'A fashion designer! That must pay you more than chicken-feed, I imagine?'

'It's very profitable,' Noelle admitted. She sighed. 'Given time and opportunity I could have done so much for poor old Claddagh, but now . . .' She shrugged. 'I suppose it's back to London, to practicalities, and forget the dreams.'

'One of which,' he guessed shrewdly, 'was to marry Fergus Carrick? By all the saints, what ails the man? Doesn't he realise what he's missing? Not only you, of course, but the money you could put into Claddagh. Together the pair of you could have put the estate on a firm footing again. I suppose,' his expression became calculating, 'he's not likely to be selling up after all? On his own, I suspect, he's not too flush with money?'

'No, he's not, but I can't see him selling, even so.' Her face brightened. 'Perhaps that's the answer. Perhaps he doesn't feel he can afford to support a wife.' The thought gave her new hope and she was eager all at once to be gone, to find Fergus, to reassure him that she wouldn't be an additional burden on his strained finances.

Her great-aunt had told her to put aside pride, and the result had been the almost overwhelming conviction that Fergus loved her. It was surely worth the potential happiness to risk that pride again? As she turned to retrace her steps, Patrick called after her, 'Don't be forgetting the celebration. Tomorrow?'

'I won't forget,' she called back, then broke into a run.

No one had seen Fergus since his abrupt departure, and Noelle was forced to curb her impatience to talk to him. Unable to relax, she spent the afternoon pacing from room to room, alert for any sound that might herald his return. There was no sign of him at dinner, a meal to which Noelle could not do justice.

Miss O'Rourke usually retired early, and that night was no exception. Thus Noelle was left alone to fill the seemingly endless hours. Surely Fergus must return tonight?

Not knowing the reasons for his anger, she found herself prey to morbid thoughts and fancies, and the later the hour grew, the more anxious she became. At last, almost too weary to stand, she made her way upstairs and prepared for bed.

She had extinguished her light when she thought she heard the faint sounds of an approaching car. Fatigue forgotten, she was out of bed in an instant and at her window which overlooked the stable yard. It was Fergus's car gliding to a halt. Only his side-lights showed, as though he avoided advertising his presence.

But Noelle had waited too long to be deterred from the confrontation she sought. Besides, by morning her courage might have evaporated.

Pulling a robe over its matching flimsy nightgown, she went barefoot down the main stairs and into the dining room. When he entered she would be ready to waylay him. She waited. Several moments elapsed, then the Hall's ancient plumbing began its usual hideous vibrations, the unmistakable evidence that one of the bathrooms was in use. Who could be bathing or showering at this hour? Only Fergus, and if so, how had he evaded her vigilance? Then she realised. He must have used the rear entrance through Siobhan's kitchen and gone up by the servants' staircase to the first floor. Fergus had been taking no chance of an encounter.

His deliberate avoidance of her only served to increase her determination. Fergus owed her an explanation of his behaviour, if nothing else.

She re-ascended the stairs and crossed the landing to his bedroom door. To avoid disturbing Miss O'Rourke during her illness, all the heavy doors on that floor had been eased, their hinges oiled, and now his door opened soundlessly under her hand. Yes, the sound of running water did come from the bathroom adjoining. Noelle seated herself in a wicker-work chair and prepared to wait once more.

It wasn't long before the interconnecting door opened and Fergus emerged, clad only in a brief robe, the towel with which he vigorously rubbed his hair obscuring his vision. Not until he passed the chair and her bare feet came within his downbent view did he realise her presence. With a muttered curse, he flung the towel from him and glared down at her.

'What the hell are you doing in my room at this time of night?'

'Waiting for you,' she said, more calmly than she felt.

'For what purpose?'

'I think you know that.'

'I've no idea.' So he wasn't going to help her at all. Noelle drew a deep breath before launching her attack.

'Today,' she said, 'you all but made love to me, all but proposed to me,' and as he remained silently enigmatic, 'didn't you?'

'Almost,' he agreed, 'but not quite.'

'You would have done,' she persisted, 'if Aunt Bridie hadn't produced that other will.'

'Maybe, maybe not.' He was still avoiding her gaze, but his would-be-casual tone had an edge of strain to it.

'Fergus!' She stood up and grasped his arm. 'Look at me! Look at me and convince me that you wouldn't have proposed if things had stayed as they were, if we'd still been joint owners of Claddagh.'

He met her eyes but his own were coldly inscrutable, only a nerve jumping in his temple betrayed his forced calm.

'What I might or might not have done is pure speculation. The facts are that I didn't ask you to marry me and that I'm not going to ask you.'

Noelle took a step backwards, feeling with one hand for the support of the chair.

'You really mean that!' It was an anguished whisper and as he turned his back on her, as if he could no longer tolerate her gaze, she grasped at the tattered remnants of her self-respect. 'You . . . you opportunist!' she hissed. 'I was right about you.

While Claddagh was half mine you had to get me to
marry you, to keep it undivided. That will turning
up was a godsend to you, wasn't it? You don't have
to marry me now, or pretend, as you were
pretending this afternoon, to have any feeling for
me. In fact you're now in a position to ask me to
leave. Well, don't trouble yourself. I'm leaving!'

She didn't wait to see if he would answer, she
didn't want to hear his voice again. Back in her
room she found all desire for sleep had fled. Instead
she spent the long, dark hours packing her
suitcases, removing from the room every evidence
of her occupation. Tomorrow, she would not only
wish Patrick Godspeed, she would be toasting her
own departure, a bitter celebration of the death of
her hopes, her love.

She came down to breakfast hollow-eyed but
composed. No traces remained of the tears she had
shed over her packing. There was no sign of Fergus,
apart from the evidence of an earlier breakfaster.

'He's gone over to the Faheys to ask Terence
Fahey's advice,' her great-aunt told her. 'He's come
to the most amazing decision. He's decided to sell
off all the horseflesh, give up the stud and
concentrate on the dairy and sheep farming. He
said horses were for rich men and mugs.'

Noelle shrugged uninterestedly. 'He's right, of
course, and he can do what he likes now, can't he?'

Miss O'Rourke looked at her with some anxiety.

'Are you very cross with me, dear?'

'For what? Concealing the will, or revealing it?
Neither. What's done is done.' Noelle's tone was

quite unlike her usually lively manner. 'Besides, I wouldn't have liked to own half of Claddagh under false pretences.'

'You would never have known,' Miss O'Rourke sighed, 'if I'd only had the courage to go through with it. But there's the next life to be considered. And I feel,' she added heavily, 'that my meddling has done more harm than good where you and Fergus are concerned.'

'No,' Noelle assured her. 'Again, I'd rather have truth than lies. As you know, once or twice Fergus did suggest a marriage of convenience. I turned him down, because I knew it wasn't a serious suggestion, and I would never agree to marry anyone on those terms. So then he thought he'd pretend to fall in love with me. He might even have steeled himself to propose, but for the alternative will.'

'There you are, you see!' wailed Miss O'Rourke. 'I have ruined everything.'

'You've ruined nothing,' firmly, 'there was nothing to ruin. Don't you think I'd have found out eventually? Fergus couldn't have kept up the pretence for ever that he loved me.'

'But I can't believe it *was* all pretence,' her aunt persisted. 'I've known the dear boy a long time and I'm sure he's in love with you, only something is holding him back.'

'And I'm sure you're wrong,' Noelle said. 'Aunt Bridie, I know this is going to upset you, but I've decided to leave Claddagh. I've no right to be here now.'

'But Noelle! Oh, my dear, of course I don't want you to go. But apart from that, you've spent so much of your time and your own money on restoring the place.'

'Not really. The money from the sale of the paintings did that. I got back my original stake.'

'But the decorating, all your hard work——!'

'Aunt Bridie,' gently, 'I don't begrudge it. I love Claddagh and I hate the idea of leaving, but what else can I do?'

'I suppose you *are* in love with Fergus?' Bridie said wistfully.

'Yes, but I intend to fall out of love with him as soon as possible.' Brave words, she thought, that could never be fulfilled. She would love Fergus Carrick for the rest of her life.

'What will you do?'

'Go back to London, cancel all my plans for Dublin, take up my work where I left off.'

'When do you plan to go, if you really must?'

'Today. Now. I've packed. I'm going to call a taxi to take me over to Galway to meet Patrick. He's leaving for England, too; I'll travel with him.'

Miss O'Rourke was thoughtful as they finished their breakfast, then:

'Don't bother with a taxi, Noelle. Use Fergus's car, he won't be needing it today; he rode over to the Faheys. Seamus can get one of the lads to drive him over later to collect it.' Seamus was the odd job man about the place, in reality past working age, but kept on for his loyalty to the family. 'I'll speak to Seamus,' Miss O'Rourke went on, 'while you collect your luggage together.'

Having accepted the idea of her departure, her

great-aunt seemed unexpectedly eager to co-operate, Noelle mused wryly as she went upstairs. She hadn't wanted tears and protestations, but she had expected more flattering resistance to her plans.

The car was drawn up at the front door when she came downstairs and Miss O'Rourke, looking mournful, saw her off. Her aunt hadn't even asked her to keep in touch, or to visit occasionally, Noelle thought bewilderedly, as she turned for a last regretful look at Claddagh Hall, its grey stone sparkling silver in the morning sunlight.

Perversely the whole countryside was looking at its loveliest, the greens richer, the browns warmer, the waters of the lough brilliantly inviting, and she was turning her back on all of it for ever. Impatiently, she dashed a hand across her eyes. It wouldn't improve things if she crashed the car and injured herself. She must look ahead, towards the resumption of work, a greater dedication than ever to her career and a day when the bitter hurt she now felt had been dulled by time.

How awful this stretch of road was, she thought a few miles further on. Every bump and pothole seemed to jar the elderly vehicle, so that she feared for damage to its chassis. But when the steering became totally unresponsive, she realised it wasn't just the road surface that was to blame. She had a flat tyre, a slow puncture.

It was a good thing Patrick wasn't expecting her so early. Until she met him he would have no idea of her revised plans.

Noelle had held a driving licence for years, so she was no dunce where the mechanics of a vehicle were concerned, but Fergus's car was old and after a while she began to wonder how long it was since the wheel-nuts had been removed. Certainly they were defeating all her efforts. Frustrated, she sat on the side of the road to rest. She looked at her watch again. It was well past lunchtime. Patrick would be thinking she'd stood him up.

Sighing, she decided to have one more try. If she were unsuccessful, she would have to lock her luggage in the car and walk to the next village in search of assistance. Perhaps it was the rest, or perhaps the wheel-nuts had been on the point of submission anyway, but this time she succeeded in removing them. She trundled the wheel to the rear of the car and opened the boot, to take out the spare tyre. It was flat.

'And they talk about women drivers!' she muttered crossly. But what did she do now?

The distant sound of another car approaching along the empty twisting road raised her spirits. She would beg a lift for herself and her luggage. Fergus could sort out the problem of his abandoned car. It would serve him right.

As the car came into sight, she stepped out into the road, hand upraised to halt the driver, and as it stopped she was surprised to recognise a familiar face.

'Suzanne? Thank goodness! I've got a puncture and the spare's useless too. You're not going into Galway by any chance?'

Suzanne leant across and opened the passenger door.

'Hop in.'

'Just a minute. I've got a couple of suitcases.' She thrust them on to the back seat. 'With a bit of luck I'll be able to catch Patrick before he gives me up.'

'Running away with Patrick Byrne?' asked Suzanne as she drove on.

'No!' Noelle laughed at the idea.

'Fergus thinks you are.'

'Oh?' Noelle looked sharply at the other girl. 'Then he knows I've left?'

'Yes. When I drove him back to Claddagh, Miss O'Rourke was waiting to pounce on him with the news.'

'And I suppose she just happened to tell him I was going to meet up with Patrick?' Noelle began to see. 'She didn't by any chance imply that we . . .?' and as Suzanne nodded, 'Well, it didn't work, did it?' Bitterly, 'He didn't come chasing after me.'

'You wanted him to?'

'Well, what do you think!' Noelle sighed, then, as she looked around her, 'Surely this isn't the road to Galway? I don't remember this stretch at all.' As they turned left at a T-junction, 'But I *do* know this bit. We're going the wrong way.'

'The wrong way for Galway and Patrick, yes, but the right way for you and Fergus.'

'He sent you? No, he wouldn't!'

'No, he wouldn't,' Suzanne agreed. 'Because whatever other faults Fergus may have, and no man is perfect, his worst failing has always been his stiff-necked pride. Miss O'Rourke sent me.'

'Then she's wasting her time, and yours. Suzanne, will you please turn around and take me to Galway. I don't know about Fergus's pride, but I have mine and . . .'

'And you think that's more important than the fact that you love Fergus . . . and that he loves you?'

'That I don't believe.'

'Fergus loves you,' Suzanne insisted, 'and if that second will hadn't turned up, there wouldn't have been any problem. He'd have been quite happy for you, as joint owner, to contribute to Claddagh's restoration. But now the place belongs to him, he's hard up, and knowing what he does . . . about you . . .'

'*What* does he know about me?' Noelle said sharply. She had forgotten her urgency to reach Galway.

'I'm afraid it was my fault,' Suzanne confessed. 'I didn't realise it was meant to be a secret. When I was in London, John took me to Noelle et Cie. He's as proud of you as if you were his own daughter.'

'And you told Fergus!'

'Yes. Oh, don't you see, Noelle? He doesn't want it thought, by you or by anyone else, that he's after your money.'

Noelle sighed, and for the first time relaxed in her seat.

'Just how sure are you that Fergus does love me?'

'As sure as this, he told me so.'

'When?'

'Weeks ago. But then he said he was very much afraid you disliked him, that he'd ruined any chances he might have had. Apparently, when you first met, he put you off with his wry sense of humour? And you've done nothing but argue since?'

'I'd like to believe you,' Noelle said slowly. 'But suppose I try to see him again and he puts me down again?'

'He won't, not if you go about it the right way.'

'What *is* the right way?' Noelle sounded despairing and Suzanne shrugged.

'Only you will know that, when the time comes. I've done all I can, and so, incidentally, has your great-aunt.' She giggled a little. 'Fancy that dear old lady being devious enough to ask Seamus to start a puncture in one tyre and let down the spare!'

'She did what?'

But before Noelle could exclaim further over Bridie O'Rourke's well-meant perfidy, Suzanne went on. 'Noelle, *will* you try? Fergus has been such a good friend to me. I don't think John and I would ever have got together but for him. He knew how much I liked John, but I wouldn't have dared to look him up in London without Fergus's moral support. I'd like to see Fergus as happy as I know I'm going to be.'

'Suzanne,' Noelle took a deep, steadying breath, 'I'll try—*how* I'll try!—and if you're right,' sudden elation swept through her, for Suzanne seemed so very positive that all would turn out well, 'if you're right, you shall have an exclusive Noelle et Cie wedding dress as my present to you.' Then, she asked, 'But do you know where Fergus is?'

The car which had been travelling more and more slowly, now stopped.

'Somewhere around here, I imagine.' Suzanne chuckled. 'I don't know what I'd have done if I hadn't persuaded you by this time. I'd have had to

drive around some more, I suppose.' She pointed
across the nearby field. 'When Aunt Bridie told him
you'd gone and that you were meeting Patrick, he
just walked away, but I knew where he'd go. He
always used to come here when he was especially
happy. But he came here too when he was troubled.'

Noelle recognised the place.

'I know it. I've been here too, once.' She opened
the door and stepped out into the road. 'Wish me
luck, Suzanne!'

'With all my heart!'

She ran down the well remembered grassy slope,
scrambled over the wall and entered the ancient
yew wood. As she came out on the far side of the
trees, her steps began to lag. Suppose Fergus
repulsed her again?

He was in almost the identical secluded spot as on
the occasion when he had brought her here. But
today he wasn't sitting looking across the lough
towards Claddagh. Instead he lay prone, and as she
approached across the sun-warmed knoll, she saw
that he had fallen asleep. He didn't even stir as she
sat down beside him.

Noelle considered his face as he slept. There were
no marks of irony or mockery now to mar the
handsome bearded face, though there were lines of
strain. In slumber the hard, ascetic planes had
softened, giving him an oddly vulnerable look. But
if she were to wake him, what then?

His unawareness of her presence was a bonus,
giving her time to steady her quivering nerves, to
plan her assault against the sturdy resistance of his

pride. But how should she proceed? The longer she studied his sleeping face, the more tender, the more urgent her feelings for him became. In his unconscious state he was totally hers; awake, verbally and physically he would undoubtedly be hostile.

'You'll know the right way to approach him when the time comes,' Suzanne had said hopefully, and all Noelle's instincts were now pointing a way. There were no written rules, after all, that said a man must make all the running. With a prayer in her heart and all her love on her warm, soft lips, she leant over him, pressing her mouth to his.

As he stirred and started, half-sleeping, half-waking, she allowed her full weight to rest across his chest, her hands holding and caressing his face and head, as her mouth became more urgent, seeking to arouse a reaction in him.

The results were beyond her imaginings. Far from denying the invasion of her mouth, the moist seekings of her tongue, his mouth opened to her, his response as sensuous, as searching as her own. His arms banded around her and tightened. He moved suddenly, rolled with her, his body assuming the dominance that briefly had been hers. His was now the ascendance, the commanding strength, the urgent demand.

'Noelle? It really is you! I thought you'd gone away,' he said wonderingly, 'that I'd lost you!'

'You're never going to lose me,' she told him lovingly, her mouth planting tender little kisses around his until he stopped her teasing and captured her lips in a long, searching kiss.

Passion mounted between them, as with unerring

sureness his hands stirred her body, holding her trapped, the warm pressure doing unimaginable things to her tingling nerves. She had been right to take him unprepared, his sun-warmed, sleep-relaxed body responding instinctively, overriding any mental reservations he might have. Trembling, she urged against the hardness of him, whispering his name, the sound vibrant with her love, her needs.

'Noelle?' His voice was husky. 'This shouldn't be happening. I didn't intend . . .'

'But *I* did,' she told him shamelessly, her fingers caressingly against the male hardness of him. 'Oh Fergus, I want you so much, love you so much, and I know now that you want me. You can't deny it. Why should we both suffer because your stupid pride won't let you admit it?'

He sighed deeply.

'Oh, I admit I want you,' he said, his voice thickened with desire, 'I've always wanted you, it seems, but how could I expect you to believe that I loved you, when all we seemed to do was fight . . . and now, when my motives can only seem self-seeking, mercenary . . .'

With a purely feline gesture, she smoothed her cheek against the harsher contours of his bearded face.

'I think *I* fell in love at first sight,' she murmured, ignoring his protests. 'I only knew that however much you annoyed me, I didn't want to go away, never to see you again.'

As her hands became more insistent in their intimacy, he drew a long shuddering breath.

'Noelle; stop! You don't know what you're doing. It's madness. I won't have it said,' he spoke unevenly, 'that I'm after your money. I've nothing to offer you, Noelle.'

'Nothing?' Her tone was scornful. 'You yourself are not nothing. Fergus, don't you know you mean everything to me, more than my career, more than Claddagh. Without you everything would be meaningless.' She began to give him convincing evidence of her words, teasing him, inviting him, until at the gentle insistence of her lips and hands she felt his desire grow and expand, until his demand was as active as her own.

'I *love* you, Fergus,' she repeated.

'And I love you,' he sighed, his lean fingers, in their turn, stroking, enjoying, until at last he raised her to merge with him, an ecstatic soaring of body and spirit, linked together in mutual fulfilment.

They lay, quietly entwined, her head against his shoulder, the occasional brief shudder of remembered joy still triggering sensitive nerve endings.

'Noelle,' Fergus whispered her name achingly, 'I'm sorry. Don't you understand? In spite of—of everything, I can't ask you to marry me. You're a rich woman, and I——'

'You're the man I love,' she insisted, 'and,' mischievously, 'you don't *have* to ask me to marry you.'

'I don't?' He sounded bewildered, affronted even. 'Then what are you suggesting, because I warn you . . .'

She laughed, secure in the knowledge of being

loved, in her newly discovered power over him.

'No. In a few weeks, we're going to throw the largest party Claddagh Hall has ever seen, for the whole neighbourhood, all our friends and relations, and if it will save your precious pride, *I'll ask you*, in front of the lot of them!'

At this he sat erect, looking doubtfully at her, at her face alight with love for him, but with mischievous intent in the blue eyes.

'I believe you really would, you shameless hussy!' Then, with sudden swift decision, he slid the ring from his finger, the sunlight glinting on the heart and clasped hands. 'To hell with pride and public opinions,' he said forcefully. 'I do my own proposing!' He took her left hand in his. 'Will you marry me, Noelle?' And as she nodded wordlessly, sudden tears of happiness filling her throat, he slid his mother's ring, the ring of Claddagh, on to the third finger of the hand he held.

For a moment he remained still, looking down at their clasped hands, then brown eyes met sparkling blue ones.

'Do you know,' he sounded as if he were enjoying the realisation, 'that's the first time I've been seduced! But now what?' And as her eyes gave him back the answer, he leant over her. 'And I'll do my own seducing, too . . . this time, anyway!'

**For the millions who can't read
Give the Gift of Literacy**

One out of five adults in North America
cannot read or write well enough
to fill out a job application
or understand the directions on a bottle of medicine.

**You can change all this by joining the fight
against illiteracy.**

For more information write to:
Contact, Box 81826, Lincoln, Neb. 68501
In the United States, call toll free: 800-228-3225

**The only degree you need
is a degree of caring**

Harlequin Romance

Coming Next Month

2845   WHEN LOVE FLIES BY Jeanne Allen
The strong sensitive man sitting beside a frightened American admires her for facing her fear of flying. But Lindsey has a greater fear—that of loving a man who, like her late father, makes a living flying planes.

2846   TEMPERED BY FIRE Emma Goldrick
She's a young doctor, planning a quiet summer of convalescence. He's an ex-military man, now writing a book and planning a peaceful summer of work. They meet in New England—and all plans for peace and quiet go up in flames!

2847   FUSION Rowan Kirby
Despite her successful career, a solicitor, whose husband deserted her and their son, feels so emotionally insecure that she struggles against getting involved again, even when she finds a man she could love.

2848   IN LOVE WITH THE MAN Marjorie Lewty
Delighted to be part of a fact-finding team of Tokyo, a computer operator's pleasure is spoiled when her big boss unexpectedly accompanies them and thinks she's an industrial spy.

2849   STAIRWAY TO DESTINY Miriam MacGregor
Delcie, a typist, tired of catering to the need of her overprotective aunts, decides to work for a renowned New Zealand author at his sheep station. There she learns about her own needs . . . as a woman.

2850   BEYOND HER CONTROL Jessica Steele
Brooke rushes to France to rescue her young sister from a case of puppy love for a worldly, wealthy chateau owner—only to fall in love with him herself!

Available in July wherever paperback books are sold, or through Harlequin Reader Service.

In the U.S.
901 Fuhrmann Blvd.
P.O. Box 1397
Buffalo, N.Y. 14240-1397

In Canada
P.O. Box 603
Fort Erie, Ontario
L2A 5X3

Take 4 best-selling love stories FREE
Plus get a FREE surprise gift!

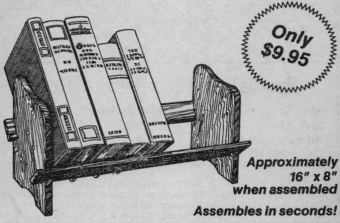